FOR ONCE

AJA

Sign up for special news, releases, and contests here:
https://bit.ly/3wYPTz4

DEAR READER

For Once was inspired by life and also a blog I penned years ago that can be found here. Carina and Salik took some time to come to me but I'm glad they did. In writing this story, I realized something: I am absolutely a fan of insta-romances. I think I prefer reading them *and* writing them. I'm sorry if you came here looking for something that would take time. I tend to get my characters *there* rather quickly because I like the idea of people knowing what they want and going for it. To be fair, however, Carina has known Salik for much longer than he's known her. That's all I'll say.

Also, quiet as it's been kept, most of my books are standalone stories. Many of them hold similar themes or have some crossover characters so they end up grouped together. For example, The Love & Passion and Love & Redemption series. Those stories while connected, can be read without reading the others. *For Once* actually has some crossover characters, one in particular. Khalil I. Berry is the main character in She's Got Soul, book 1 of my Soulmates series. You do not have to read that series to get the gist of this story but it's a GREAT series, so I recommend you take the time to purchase or download the books.

Last note: This is a millennial love story. One that includes some colorful words (nasty, profane) from time to time. I don't apologize for telling these characters' story just the way they gave it to me.

Love & Light,

Aja

DEDICATION

To him.
For the love.
For the inspiration.
For planting his love inside me.

And …
To the underdog.
Your time for love is coming.
Just believe.

For Once

Aja

She Loves Words Publishing, LLC

© Aja Graves 2021

All rights reserved.

Cover Design: Young Creations

No part of this book may be reproduced in any form or by any means without the prior consent of the publisher, except for brief quotes used in reviews.

This is a work of fiction. Any references or similarities to actual events, real people, living or dead, or to real locales are intended to give the novel a sense of reality. Any similarity in other names, characters, places, and incidents is entirely coincidental.

BLURB

Carina Clark had been on the dating scene for longer than she cared to admit. It had been such an unsuccessful journey, that she was absolutely, positively done with it. Until sexy Salik ... and his offer to take her out to see one of her favorite vocalists. She figured, at the very least, she'd enjoy good music and his smile, but definitely not more. Why would she want that? Men never stayed past a toss in the sheets.

But things take a turn that night and Salik ... he actually stayed long enough for coffee in the morning.

For once, one stayed.

For Once is a sexy love story and a standalone.

FOR ONCE: THE PLAYLIST

"Do I hand the coochie over, or my heart? I want someone to take care of boffum to be honest. " - Carina

CARINA

"Yeah, you like that, don't you? You like this dick in your pussy."

The room was dark but not so dark where I couldn't see the outline of Richie's bearded face hovering over mine—not to mention the warmth of his breath pelted against my cheek as he panted over top of me reminding me that I was not alone in my bed. My body slid up and down my expensive Egyptian cotton sheet due to his forceful pumping. If not for that, I might have forgotten what we were doing because the inner parts of me still hadn't woken up yet.

"Carina, baby, I ain't hear you. You like that?"

He wasn't going to stop asking me questions until I answered, so I managed to fake my pleasure.

"Mmmmhmmm, this is good."

When he responded with, "Yeah, that's what I thought," I rolled my eyes and hoped that it was in fact dark enough that he didn't see that.

I lied to the man; I know. Sue me. Faking orgasms took women back thousands of years, I knew that too, but sometimes it was the only solution to this problem. I knew he would never get me there, so why not tell the man what he needed to hear so we could both go to sleep? And I know you might be wondering why I was wasting my time having sex with Richie when every one of the other times we've had sex, I've been less than satisfied. The answer was simple: I was hoping a miracle would happen and that one of these times, I'd come away with what he walked away with. An orgasm.

I met Richie about six months ago at a charity function at my sister's job. Tori was a pediatrician at the Children's Hospital, and they were auctioning off Lego sets. The sets would go to the children, not to us, but the money earned also went to the ward being built for children with advanced-stage Chronic lymphocytic leukemia. Richie and I auctioned on the same Batman Lego set, and we were competitive about it too, but Richie had his sights set on getting to know me, so he let me win the set and asked to take me out to ease his broken heart over losing.

It was a corny pickup which should have been the first red flag I paid attention to. The second should have been him taking me out to Applebee's instead of someplace truly impressive for a first date. And I'm saying this from a sincere place—it's not the amount of money. Cost-efficient dates are cool; I've even been taken places that were free beyond the cost of parking; however, sometimes, a man providing little to no effort was an indicator of things to come. Pun intended.

Richie could not make me cum if I placed my clit at the tip of his dick. It really was a sad situation. Yet, I still responded to his out-of-the-blue "wyd" texts, which almost always resulted in him coming over late that night and with him leaving before I even tossed over.

I looked over at the clock on my nightstand. 10:05. I needed sleep, and I needed it now. I shifted my hips a little to let him know I wanted to change positions and placed my legs on his shoulders. He groaned like he was going to get busy, but as expected, three pumps later, his mouth formed in the shape of an O, and his face contorted like he had a leg cramp. Then he lost control, as I had hoped for, and came inside of the rubber. Less than an hour later, Richie gave me his usual line about needing to get up early so he had to leave blah blah blah. Yeah, yeah, get going. I didn't need his platitudes or his lies anymore. I knew what was up.

Being in this cycle with Richie was no one's fault but mine. I settled with what I had instead of waiting to get what I truly wanted and needed out of a man. He grew on me as well, and that was usually my downfall. If I liked someone even a little bit, I started to see the good in situations that were dead, tired and washed up. I'd have a vice grip on that situation until it was clear there wasn't any more good to see in the person. My closest friends and family always said it was my biggest flaw—that I was too nice—and where was the lie?

I've always led with my heart.

I was the little girl that didn't mind sharing with my sister, Tori, and my brother, Yusef. I wanted them happy, even if for a moment it made me unhappy. Later I was told this was *middle child's syndrome* and the need to be a people pleaser. I didn't know anything about having a condition behind my apparent flexibility. I only knew one of them wanted something I had, and it would make them happy if I handed it over or, at the very least, broke off a piece for them. The same could be said for friendships. My childhood friends never had to worry that I wouldn't let them play with the dopest Barbie I possessed. In my mind, I would be able to play with her when they left my house. Why not allow them this happiness? It would be later that I learned most other people weren't like this. They didn't like to share, and in fact, they went out of their way to make sure you didn't get the things you wanted if they wanted it as well.

Take for instance, the app developer job I applied for a month ago. I knew that Charlene Plasky was interested in it as well, but after one of our team lunches, she pulled me aside outside the breakroom after I threw my trash out.

"I know you are going to put in for the job up on 49." Forty-nine was the floor for the app developers. She and I worked on the fiftieth floor, where we ran data and quality checks on the software that was being developed.

I nodded and wondered why her ice blue eyes kept darting around like she was sharing something top secret.

"I'm just letting you know that I applied too, but I think you're more deserving."

Who says that to someone they are supposedly competing against?

"Oh, okay. Well, I think you're deserving too. You're qualified, right?"

Eyes darted around again, and then she looked me square in the eye and admitted, "Honestly, no. I still need to complete one of the assessments online, but I'm hoping my connections can get me through." That's who says something like that because damn right, I was more deserving. The fuck!

Do you ever have to work hard to keep your face expressionless? No, just me?

"Well, good luck with that, Charlene."

That was all I had for her before leaving her standing there with that damn smug look on her face. I had better things to do, like trying to get the job I wanted, with my hard work, determination, and blessings from Above.

The following morning, no less sexually frustrated than I was before Richie answered *my* "wyd" text, I got to work wondering when I was going to find a man that gave me everything I wanted for once. I had no plans on looking for him, but damn, could he just show up? Good hearts deserved some loving. *And a breakfast sandwich,* I thought as I eyed the kiosk inside of my work building.

The KIB building is where KIB Enterprises were headquartered. The company's founder and CEO, Khalil I. Berry, wanted a space that made it easy for the working person. In addition to food being served from seven in the morning to three in the afternoon, there was an on-site gym, day care center, meditation space, and even a park located behind the silver skyscraper. He even bought the space next to the building and turned it into a parking structure so that he could control the prices, making it more affordable for his employees to park on site every day. KIB was a great place to work, and the breakfast sandwiches were a highlight of my morning. They weren't my favorite sandwiches in the whole wide world, but Tony did a good enough job to keep me coming back here every day.

Just as I approached, I saw Salik Gregory get in line. Even from this view of his back, you could tell this man was finer than frog hair. Just delicious. His height allowed him to tower above the other people going to their respective work locations. His muscular build set him apart from most of the men moving about around him. Even the security guards that worked here were no match for Salik. His strong biceps made me envision him hoisting me in the air while handling me in so many delicious ways. It was a fantasy because Salik didn't even know I existed, but I knew exactly who he was, I thought as I licked my lips. *Girl, you're horny.* I couldn't deny that that was a big part of my thoughts this morning, needing someone to make me fall apart from great sex. But it was more than that. He fascinated me for some reason.

Most days, I would make it here in just enough time to see him grab the same thing: a smoothie and oatmeal or something like that. I was usually a few people behind him, and that allowed me to watch him perform his morning routine without him detecting me. Not that I was hiding. I just knew Salik was off-limits for a good reason, but I could look without touching, right?

Those were my thoughts as I approached the kiosk to stand behind him in line. Part of me wanted to find a reason to speak, but any attempt would have come off cheesy. That was until I saw him patting his pockets as if he couldn't find his wallet or keys.

SALIK

I had a reputation for being the office hoe at KIB Enterprises. It's a reputation that will probably never leave me while I work here, even though I was working hard to show I was a different man now. I made some mistakes when I first started working here, and those mistakes followed me almost everywhere I went these days.

I doubt this is what Khalil, or Mr. Berry, expected when he recruited me at a barbershop three years ago. I'd been going to *Marlon's* for more nearly a decade at that point and had never met one of Pittsburgh's wealthiest black men that also frequented the barbershop I'd been going to. *Marlon's* had been open for nearly twenty years, serving a large part of this community with the freshest cuts along with a side of Marlon's wisdom. Marlon wasn't the only good barber in this mid-size storefront shop; the other barbers that had chairs in there were all good, so even if I couldn't get in with Marlon himself, it was still safe to sit in anyone's chair. One Saturday a few years ago, I headed over to *Marlon's*, not for my cut, but about some work I did for a couple of his customers. Khalil Berry, who I knew from all the online articles about him and his company, was in Marlon's chair when I arrived to drop off some computers I worked on for Chad and Tariq. After I went over a few things with the guys about firewalls, virus/malware software, and avoiding porn sites, they paid me for the repairs, which would help me pay off the student loans from my tuition at CMU. In between receiving my degree, I would get jobs at tech companies but there seemed to be a glass ceiling for employees that looked like me. My degree and my skillset deserved more space to grow and shine. I was only waiting for the right opportunity to come along and by time I hit thirty years old, I started to believe that would never happen.

I had heard Mr. Berry had been coming here since he was a teenager but never ran into him. I imagined him pulling up to the curb in a sleek limo with a suited driver helping him out of his car, and only once the shop had been cleared of us commoners, but today was the busiest day of the week. It was packed in here. And I saw no limo outside waiting either.

He and Marlon were huddled together, chuckling at something I couldn't make out, but it wasn't my business to know what it was, so I gathered my things to get on with the rest of my day. Just as I was getting ready to slide out, Marlon called out to me, "Hey, not so fast, Salik. Get on over here."

Now don't get me wrong, meeting someone like Khalil Berry, mega-millionaire, close to billionaire, brotha, and who my mom called Rico Suave, was a dream come true for a nerd like myself. I just wasn't prepared for something this big. I always thought dressing in my one good suit would be a requirement to meeting someone so pivotal. I didn't need a narrator telling me what was about to go down. Make no mistake about it; even sitting there in dark blue jeans and a charcoal gray sweater rocking Timbs, he looked like money. Even my broke ass knew Brunello Cucinelli when I saw it, and this is whom I had to approach in my Levi's jeans and Ralph Lauren polo. I could tell already that Marlon was calling me over there to meet someone who had the influence to take me from working on community computers to working on the world's mainframes, which was my dream. Everyone in here knew it, especially Marlon. Marlon coached everyone who sat in his chair. From pulling *good* women, even if Marlon himself always had women problems, he used his experiences to steer us in a different direction. His advice ranged from relationships, to how to maintain basic hygiene. We trusted him here, and I did too. Marlon always had an answer or a way to get to it through a series of questions.

Talking to Mr. Berry that day made me aspire for more than just the job I wanted; it made me want his life. He was poise but down to earth, and he had a family. He was proof that a black man could have it all, even if it was a rare thing.

However, I found myself distracted off my path. I was feeling myself more than a little bit after my paychecks more than doubled and life seemed to get a little easier for me. I had always had my looks going for me anyway. Women told me I looked like Laroyce Hawkins—the guy that plays Kevin Atwater on Chicago PD. I couldn't disagree because I could be his fraternal twin or cousin, somebody. Anyway, my looks often started conversations with women, and that ultimately led to that old familiar road that has lengthened my sexual conquest list. My job should have been off-limits, but truthfully it seemed difficult to say no to the women. There they were, there I was. We spent a lot of time in the same building, sharing space, running into each other, that falling into bed after work came naturally. What didn't come as naturally was breaking what *I* thought was just a sex thing off. They started feeling things I had no idea would appear. Like how do you go from smiling, flirting, then fucking to angry that I don't want more than that? What is *more* to what we started? It never included anything in-depth. Me commenting under a few IG pics, or texting sporadically after work, wasn't a relationship by any means. So, when we did what I thought was the whole point, have sex, I figured we'd be good. Wrong. Tasha, Meena, Danielle, Patience who was far from patient, by the way. Wendy, Essence, Sandra, Trina, LuLu; all of them had an issue with me in the KIB building. Coming to work now was like facing a hostage situation every single damn day, and I had no one else to blame but myself.

My boys wondered why I didn't quit, but shiiiiit, I made close to six figures here, *and* I worked for a black man. It didn't get any better than that at my level of experience. There were too many opportunities for advancement that would be like shooting myself in the foot, and I wasn't about crippling myself any further. So about six months ago, I decided to change my behavior—no new workplace women. I'd been managing that just fine despite the fact that all the, albeit true, rumors had women approaching me left and right. "Hi, Salik" sounded an awful lot like,

"Please fuck me," to be honest. But I ignored the mind trick until this morning.

I was at the kiosk in the lobby ordering my strawberry banana smoothie and overnight oats with blueberries before taking the escalators to the elevators. Tony took my order, and it was when I went to pay that I realized I had left my wallet in my gym bag in my truck.

"Shit."

"How much is it?" I heard someone ask.

I turned towards the soft, husky voice only to find probably the most beautiful woman I'd ever seen—no exaggeration. She was shorter than I am by at least a foot, which was not exactly notable given I was six-four and a half. Her hair was very thick, shiny, and looked like it was heavy on her shoulders. Her skin was a warm latte, eyes a chestnut brown with long thick eyelashes, lips moist and pouty. Damn.

"You alright?" She asked me, her eyebrows pushed together as if she was deeply concerned. It was then that I realized I was a staring idiot.

I cleared my throat. "Yeah. I'm good."

"How much is it?" she asked me again, her eyes moving towards the counter.

I turned and eyed Tony, who smirked a little before telling Ms. Beautiful, "It's five sixty-two."

She started digging in a big red wallet she held in her hand and pulled out a ten-dollar bill like she was about to pay for my food. Like I wasn't a man who could handle my own business. Pretty or not, women didn't pay for my food.

Before I could tell her not to worry about it, she was stepping around me in her cute little peep-toe heels and handing Tony the crisp bill to pay for my items and her chai tea.

She turned to me just as I was getting my voice back. "You didn't have to do that." I wanted to say more, but I was still stunned by how gorgeous she was. All the women I encountered had nothing on her.

"No, I didn't but seeing you pat at your pockets for five bucks seemed cruel. Tony could have let you slide, I'm sure."

"He sure could have. I'm here every day at 7:45

am on the dot." Now that I thought about it, I felt a little indignant.

"I know."

My eyes went to hers before she looked away like she was embarrassed by the admission. I had never noticed her before this moment, and she knew my schedule. How is that even possible? Tony cleared his throat, and both she and I looked to see a line forming behind us. I reached out and grabbed my food off the counter while avoiding the smirk on Tony's face and we moved away from the five or so other employees clearly annoyed with us. I ignored them too.

"Well, I should let you go ... but wait, which floor do you work on?"

Her eyebrows rose above her almond-shaped eyes. "You know, so I can give you your money back."

She chuckled, and I enjoyed the way her eyes sparkled.

"Not necessary. I could spare a few bucks."

"Nah, I can't let your good deed go like that."

She chewed on her luscious lip, making me wish I could be her teeth. *Damn, what the fuck was wrong with me?*

"Pay it forward. Tomorrow, pay for the person's

food in front of you." She said it so simply I could only nod, but that wasn't what I really wanted. I wanted a chance to talk to her longer. Find out her name, at least.

Before I could say more or even find out her name, she moved towards the escalators and went up. I watched her for a few moments to see if she'd look back, but she didn't. It gave me time to observe the way her peach dress fit her bottom. Her ass was round and lush. Even her breasts looked to be more than a handful. Full figured woman, just the way I liked them. *Take a deep breath, man.* I ignored my own voice, however, and I stood there looking like a fool until people started moving around me to get up to their floors. Eventually, I did the same, wondering the whole time how I became a sucker and how I would find a way to talk to her again.

CARINA

There was a reason my philosophy was to look and not touch when it came to the man I just helped. Salik had been deemed the office slut—the guy you stayed away from if you didn't want to be talked about right along with him. My whole division knew it. His name and his many conquests, at least the loud ones, had made it around the lunchroom plenty of times when I was trying to grab my food and dip back out to eat at my desk. At first, I was intrigued by anyone that could cause such an uproar. Not because I wanted to try him or anything, but just because I always had a thing for unconventional people, men especially. Did I end up happier for it? No, but it was fun. Moreover, who could say no to a bad boy? Not me. I already told y'all my problem with saying no. Usually, the murmurs started with smiles, laughter, and teasing about what they would experience the night each and every one of them planned to go out with him. A week after that, the tone would be hostile, sometimes teary confessions of how he was a dog and shouldn't make promises he couldn't keep. So yeah, no. I didn't need him coming to find me on the fiftieth floor to hand me some change back. I think the fuck not.

But ... and I can say this here because it's a safe place ... the man is so fucking fine. Like maybe the finest of them all in this building, and that's saying a whole darn lot because Kahlil Berry went above and beyond making the place a diverse workplace. In fact, though no one said it, he was preferential to making sure young black men and women, people who looked like him and his wife, were the ones that got opportunities to be here. Sure, you were hired because you were qualified, but he wanted to make sure we knew this was a safe place to come and bring our talent. There were even STEM outreach programs funded by KIB in order to funnel young people, usually at a disadvantage, through programs that might push those young people into his company.

So when I say Salik was finer than all the brothers I see day in and out, I mean it. Think Laroyce Hawkins from Chicago PD but with even more sex appeal. *Lawd.* Even still, I would not be fantasizing about him or his soft kissable lips and what they might feel like wrapped around a nipple or my clit. Absolutely not! But again, there was still something captivating about him. For the few moments we stood face to face, I didn't see a monster that these women accused him of being in front of me, or a snake, not a dog, either. He'd been called those names and worse. I saw a *man.* Again, I know a big part of that was me always seeing the good in people and situations, and that had a way of always biting me in my big ass, but every once in a while, I was right about people, and I felt that I was right about him. Not that he wasn't a dog, but that it was all that he was. I just had no plan to find out whether I was using my psychic-good-in-people skills. Some things would have to be a mystery.

"Carina, Hello. Earth to Carina." A set of fingers appeared in front of my face and started snapping. It was Tracey. She was the only person at work that I really messed with. We occasionally hung out outside of office hours, but most of the time, we kept each other company around here. She kept me apprised of what was going on when I wasn't paying attention, and I tended to update her on the emails she refused to read because they were pointless, even if they contained some pertinent information. We were the perfect balance at work. If not for her, the days would move more slowly, and truly, I might lose my mind here. The trade-off: she was also nosey.

"Girl, quit it. I'm here."

"Where'd you zone off to, though?" She was settling into the only visitor's chair that could fit into my cube space.

"Oh, nowhere. I have a ton of work to do today. That's all." I looked everywhere but into her eyes.

I could feel her looking at me curiously, but she left it alone … for the moment.

"Girl, I came over here to tell you about my date Saturday night, but you are too busy thinking about allllllll the work you got to do, so I'll tell you another time." She rolled her eyes, and I did the same.

"Shut up and spill it."

"I thought so. Nebby Debbie." She was smiling like whether I wanted to know or not, she would have told me anyway. When she flipped her box braids over her shoulder, I could tell that this storytelling would be the highlight of her morning.

"Okay, so boom … we hit it off over dinner. I was kinda surprised about that."

"Why is that?"

"Honestly, because I only went out with him to have sex."

"You a mess, girl."

"What's the issue? You should try it sometime."

"How about, no."

"How about when was the last time you got some good dick?"

"Well …"

"Richie don't count. I already know it's whack."

"It is … wait, how do you know it's wack?"

She looked down at her short, manicured nails and then back up at me as if she had been holding onto the secret for so long, she could not wait for the moment to spill it.

I groaned. "You're my girl. You're supposed to tell me if I'm going down a familiar road."

"Okay, then if that's the case. *Salik* is a familiar road."

I cleared my throat and picked up my abandoned cellphone. I hadn't done my usual social media scrolling and now seemed like the perfect time. How is it that she knew every damn thing?

"Aht aht. Don't do that, heaux."

"Who you calling a heaux?"

"You a heaux if you get with Salik just to see if it's as good as everyone else says it is."

"What do you say?"

She made a big show of acting like she had to think about it, and I held my breath as I waited.

"Never had it."

"Well, what's the "familiar road" you talking about?" I was slowly releasing a relieved breath.

"Bitch, we might be the only two heauxs that haven't been down that road. Isn't that familiar enough?"

I wouldn't tell her that finding out she hadn't been down Salik's streets pleased me more than a little bit. I didn't even want to identify the why about that either. For now, I would just inwardly cheer about it.

"I'm not sure why you keep bringing Salik up. When have I ever said I was trying to get with him?"

"You didn't have to. I saw the way you were looking at him downstairs at the kiosk."

I had to wonder how many other people saw me trying my best not to flirt with the sexiest man in the building.

"Oh."

"Yeah, oh."

"That was nothing. The man left his wallet somewhere, so I helped him out."

"Mmmmhmmm. I bet you wanted to help him out with more than his lost wallet." Her lips were twisted, and she rolled her eyes.

"Hush."

"I'm just saying, Carina. Tell me I'm lying, and I'll walk away."

"Fine. He's finer than anyone has a right to be, but I'm not trying to hand him more than a breakfast smoothie."

She just looked at me.

"Seriously. That was all it was. Me helping someone who needed it. I didn't even tell him where I worked so he could give me my money back."

She looked at me sideways like she didn't believe me.

"Fine. You don't have to believe me. I know the truth. Salik is a distant memory or will be as soon as you get to work, and so do I."

SALIK

I've seen a ton of movies that I watched with women I was trying to get with, mind you, where two people meet, have a vibe, but don't get each other's numbers. Soon afterward, they regret it, but some act of serendipity brings them together as if the odds didn't matter. I always rolled my eyes when I saw those flicks because what are the chances of that happening in real life.

Here I was wishing something like that would happen to me and whatever her name was that worked in my building—a woman I'd never seen before. If I had, I would have never made the now crazy vow to not sleep with anyone else that worked in this building. I should have been more specific and said that I wouldn't sleep with anyone in my *department.* That was more realistic. But here I was trying to devise some plan to find out who the hell she was while also trying to focus on work. Everything on my calendar today bothered me because most of my attention was spent scrolling through the employee directory, hoping I would come across her picture.

The meeting my team had late this morning would have easily been dealt with in an email memo, but instead, Sarah, who loved face-to-face interaction, spent an hour going over the logistics of a project we all knew how to complete in our sleep. Most times, Sarah meant well, but other times it seemed as if she were checking off some sort of list required by management because the meetings were aggravating. If not for the entertainment I got from Dom, I would probably fall asleep. I had a habit of slipping off into some sleep when bored. I have been that way since I was a boy in church with my Mama.

"All of this could have been in a memo."

"I was thinking the same thing."

Dom leaned in, and I tried to ignore her dark brown mounds peeking out from the low-cut tank top. Though she had a blazer over the top, it did nothing to hide that Dom, short for Dominique Perry, had one of the most banging bodies in the building. I was one of the few that knew just how much. Dom, unlike the other women I had had sex with at work, didn't go acting all weird afterward. She wanted dick to scratch an itch she had after a bad breakup, or at least that is what she said when she approached me about hooking up. I was available, so we hit it off. Simple as that.

"Hey, eyes up here." Her smirk let me know she liked that I was looking, and I inwardly groaned. Yeah, she was cool about our roll around the bed, but she was still trying to get back to it whether she said so or not, and honestly, even if I didn't have my

"rule" in place, I wouldn't be interested. The sex was just okay, and okay was not enough to want to do it again. She was proof that a banging body did not equal banging sex.

"Sorry, my mind was actually elsewhere."

"Mmmmhmmm, on who?"

That was the other thing; Dom seemed to always want to know who I was dealing with, particularly the ones in the building. I could never prove it, but after a while, I suspected she would check out whoever I seemed to be making my move on, but when she and I were around each other, she never let on that she was a stalker, so I let it go. Now that I was done dealing in the work pool, I had no reason to worry about it. Still, there was no way I would share my curiosity about my angel from this morning.

"Not whom, what. We have a lot to do between this project and our individual assignments. Plus, I have a computer to deal with and get back to someone."

"At the barbershop?"

"Yeah."

"Maybe one day I can go with you and help you out." If I were only paying attention to the tone of her voice, I would think she was talking absent-mindedly, but her eyes held expectation. Hope.

First of all, we never did things together unless it was grabbing a drink, and really, I slowed down on that for the obvious reasons of a sexy woman and alcohol being a bad mix. Second of all, you don't take women to the barbershop unless you're making some kind of statement. The barbershop was a sacred place for most men. And in addition to that, I was too busy living my life to keep bringing my work life into my free time. So, Dom and I hadn't had drinks for a while. Work is where we conducted our friendship. The less I complicated things with any woman at work, and the better things would be for me.

"Sure. Maybe some time we can," I lied.

She gave me a smile that said she believed me, and while she went back to her notes to prepare for this meeting, I felt a sense of unease. What was happening here? The one time we had sex wasn't enough of an experience for her to get attached to is what I had convinced myself when we decided we could remain work buddies. She always seemed to do well with that, but now I wasn't so sure. I didn't have much time to deliberate on it though, because Sarah was ready to talk about something pertaining to my job here.

"Okay, guys, let's talk about where we are with the mass integration of the *Soul Match* app with the *Soul Life* app. John, you said we are close to configuring the platform where *Soul Match* can just be plugged in, right?"

"Yes, Sarah. Salik and I were playing around with some code just to run multiple modules to see what would be stable come launch. We have a few more tests to run, but we should be able to show you final specs by next Friday."

John looked to me like he hoped I would add something. Instead, I nodded because there was nothing more for me to say at this point. The truth was, we were already done running our tests, but we both decided we would halt on sharing that with Sarah or anyone else because we'd learned that these meetings often revealed something new that would either land us at square one or close enough to it and sharing our progress was a waste of time.

"That's good to know. The reason I wanted to meet today was to share something that just came down the pipeline that might impact the work you're doing now."

John and I exchanged looks and then focused on Sarah's monologue. Each word made me want to grumble out my frustration. Even though we expected changes all the way up to launch day, it didn't change the fact that we were doing four to five times the work necessary to complete the project. When the meeting was over, I got up, planning to catch John before he left the conference room but was interrupted when Dom placed her hand on my arm. I looked at her and waited for her to explain what the hell she was doing. Way too intimate at work, Dom!

"Hey ... I meant it about the barbershop or anywhere else, really. I want to hang out sometime."

I nodded and waited for her to remove her palm from me.

"I hear you. I'll let you know."

She wanted to be more than friends.

I had to figure out how I would handle things with Dom, but it wasn't a priority at the moment; work was. After meeting up with John to discuss our new approach, I headed out to lunch, making sure I avoided the spots I knew Dom frequented.

CARINA

Trying to be cute and ordering *only* a chai tea in front of Salik proved problematic as the morning wore on. I should have gone on and ordered my usual BLT croissant breakfast sandwich, and I wouldn't be hungry as a horse. Then on top of that, I had forgotten my lunch on my kitchen counter when I left out this morning, most likely due to spending so much time wondering why I wasted my coochie on Richie. Therefore, by ten o'clock, I was hungry, very hungry, and I didn't even have a cracker in my desk drawer to hold me over. By eleven o'clock, my stomach could be heard by Pat, who worked in the cube beside mine.

I heard her seat creak before she called out from her side of the partition, "Girl, if you don't just go on ahead and take a break for lunch. The whole floor can hear your stomach sounding like a tractor is coming in to demolish us all."

I groaned from my side. "It's too early. I'll be hungry by three again, and I have yoga after work."

"And? You gonna die before yoga if you don't eat. I'll cover for you if Sharise comes by asking why you're not at your desk.'"

Sharise was our supervisor, and while she was mainly cool, she tended to be unpredictable and occasionally a micromanager, which threw us all off guard. I mean, either you trust us to work through these projects you've given us the specs for, or you don't. It can't be both. But it was too early in the day to know which mood Sharise was in, so Pat was doing me a solid.

"Bless your heart and your stomach, Pat."

She chuckled. "No, bless your stomach with some food. Now go." I heard her chair creak again as she moved back to her desk to do work.

I didn't argue with her. I hurried and grabbed my small red clutch purse, my phone, and my earbuds from off my desk and practically ran to the elevator, hoping no one from my department would see me. If I moved quickly enough, I could beat the early lunch rush from all the downtowners. Happy for my low wedge-heeled peep toes sandals that allowed me to swiftly move down Liberty without much hassle, I made my way into *Trello's* and found it was mostly quiet inside. The lighting was dim enough to feel intimate, and there were plenty of tables empty, proving I made the right decision to leave when I did.

A young waiter approached and signaled to the tables with his head.

"You can take whichever table you'd like. I'd recommend that corner over by the window. It'll make it easy to get out of here when it starts to fill up in a few minutes." His smile was kind as if he were new here and hadn't learned that these people downtown would chew you up and spit you out, making you regret being a waiter. I knew it because it was a job I had while paying for school.

Giving him a grateful smile, I headed right where he suggested because it was where I was planning to sit anyway. Whenever I dined alone, I always requested to be seated closer to the front of a restaurant. Being seated in the back would make it easy for someone to grab me and take me outback. At least that's what my PaPa always told my sister and me. He insisted Tori, and I remember all the things he told us growing up so that no matter whether I had a man or not, we'd remain as safe as we could without him protecting us.

The waiter that helped me to choose a table approached and took my order.

"Ma'am, do you know what you want to order?"

I hurried to browse the simple menu. "Uh, I'll take the grilled chicken platter with basmati rice and steamed broccoli."

"Perfect. Would you like anything to drink?"

"Just water with lemon on the side, please."

"You got it."

He put his pencil and pad away inside of his black waist apron and went to the back. I watched him for a moment and captured the eyes of a man about my age in the corner off near the back. He smiled, and I smiled back politely before looking away and out the window. Maintaining eye contact often was misunderstood as an invitation, which was totally unfair. Men could look at women openly, gazing at all of us, even to the point of making us uncomfortable, and most of the time, we went on with our lives. But for them, nah, if we looked, they treated us as if we directly asked for them sex.

Downtown at this hour reminded me of that sliver of light that appeared on the horizon right before the sun revealed its full glory. You knew what was coming; you just had to wait for it. I started to put my earbuds in when the waiter, Todd, he said, brought me my water with lemon before he disappeared again. Just as I squeezed a lemon quarter into my water, I heard a familiar voice from this morning.

"Looks like someone wants us to keep bumping into each other."

I looked up and found Salik standing over the table where I was seated, and as I took in his face and his glorious body in his grey button up top and relaxed gray slacks, I had to wonder if he looked better than this morning because instantly I was thinking, *screw looking and not touching, Carina. Touch that man. Touch him all over.*

Aloud I said, "Looks like. I thought I would fly undetected away from the workplace, but work is following me, it seems."

"Looks like it."

Todd chose this moment to show up with my food and looked between Salik and me as he slid my hot plate in front of me.

"Will you be joining the lady or sitting elsewhere?"

Salik raised a thick eyebrow at me as if waiting for my verdict. There was no way I would turn him away. Not with my nipples perking up. My body was already making a decision, and I was always told to listen to my gut, and since my tits laid on my gut without a bra, I figured I should listen to them too. So, I offered him the seat across from me. "He's joining me, Todd."

"Perfect." Todd liked to say perfect. I, on the other hand, wasn't sure it *was* indeed perfect as my nipples weren't the only affected part of me. All of a sudden, as Salik folded his large body down into the wooden chair across from me, only showing how ill-equipped the furniture was for people not of average size, I was feeling hot and nervous.

"I'll give you a few minutes to look over the menu, Sir," Todd said to Salik, who shook his head.

"No need. Give me water, a coke, and a Rueben with sweet potato fries."

"Perfect. I'll be back with your drinks."

"Dude likes saying perfect," he observed as he watched Todd walk away before focusing his attention back on me.

"I was just thinking the same thing." We smiled at each other.

"Go on and eat while your food is hot. We got time to chat."

I nodded and said grace before picking up my fork to take my first bite. When I looked up at him, his eyes were focused on me so intently my cheeks felt hot. I knew I was turning red which was not a good look as far as I was concerned.

"What is it?" Never had I felt self-conscious about eating in front of a man. I had always had a healthy appetite, part of why I was taking yoga now, but enjoying my food wasn't something I would be ashamed of, so no matter what if I liked my food, I ate it.

"Nah, don't do that. Eat your food and enjoy it," he said, reading my thoughts. "It's just not often I see people stop to thank the Creator for the food in front of them anymore."

"Oh." I didn't know what else to say as I scooped up some of my rice on my fork and shoveled it in my mouth.

"Sorry if I made you uncomfortable."

"That's okay," I said around my food before finishing up chewing. "I thought you were one of those guys that hated when women ate their food."

His chuckle made my stomach tighten. "Listen, I'm about to bust my sandwich open. You should definitely do the same to your grub."

I grinned before cutting into my chicken and taking a bite. Trying to ignore the thought of what on me he could bust wide open.

"Besides, I heard the guys that did that were complaining about their dates ... we're not on a date, are we?"

I started to cough, and he smiled and picked up my water, and handed it to me. Our fingers brushed as I secured my grip on my glass, and awareness took hold of me as our eyes connected. He cleared his throat as if he felt it too and needed to break from it.

"Sorry about that."

"I'm beginning to think you like to catch me off guard."

"That's unfair. It was *you* that made your presence known to *me* this morning. You came into my life, and I'm repaying the favor."

"How so?"

"Isn't it obvious? Lunch is on me uh ... shoot. I don't even know your name."

"My name is Carina. And shame on you."

"For what?" His smirk was so damn sexy.

"For not knowing my name."

"You didn't tell me your name. So, shame on you."

"You didn't ask, and you're sitting at *my* table."

He was nodding his head. "That's true. Want me to leave?" He said it softly as if he really wanted to know. As if he would leave if I asked him to. I didn't want him to go, however, and made sure he knew it by shaking my head. He smiled and sat back in a relaxed pose just as Todd returned with his food and his drinks on a platter.

As our waiter took care placing the items in front of Salik, I watched him while making a note of how big he was, how fine he was, how I liked his energy. Then, as if he felt me staring at him, he returned my gaze and didn't let go. I was keenly aware of Todd watching us, but instead of asking if we were okay, he promptly disappeared.

"Perfect," Salik murmured. I wasn't sure if he was referring to Todd leaving us alone or the food placed in front of him. I didn't care. I only agreed that this was in fact, perfect.

I watched as he said his grace and smiled as he started on his fries. Now I got it; he was a praying man. We ate in silence a few moments before he took a moment to drink some water.

"How long have you worked at KIB, Carina? Pretty name, by the way."

His compliment warmed me, but I held onto that. "It'll be three years this October. How about you?"

"Three years this August."

"So, we came in at the same time practically."

"Yes, and we never met. I wonder why."

I shrugged. "It's a big building with lots of people. I've heard of you though."

His expression changed. "I'm sure you have. Is that why you helped me this morning?"

I looked at him with confusion. "Huh?"

"Usually, the rumors make women throw themselves at me."

I worked to contain my anger. What had I been saying about his energy? Well, I was wrong apparently.

"Uh no. I helped you because you seemed to need it and sparing five bucks is far from what I'd think is a sexual gesture. Is that all you're worth?"

That got his attention. He put his hands up, and his eyes looked apologetic.

"You're right. I shouldn't have jumped to conclusions."

"Damn right you shouldn't have." Suddenly, the rest of my food seemed unappealing. I started looking around as if all my belongings weren't just sitting in my lap waiting for a moment like this where I would need to rush to make my escape.

His large palm engulfed mine on top of the table, holding me there until I looked up at him. "Please stay, Carina. I sincerely apologize."

Taking a deep breath, I summoned calm. If I had rumors flying around about me as much as he had, true or not, I suppose I would have a chip on my shoulder. A woman being labeled a slut was derogatory. A man on the other hand, was assumed to like that kind of attention, and that was unfair. So, I relaxed and gave him a small smile.

"I'll stay but only because I want to see you pay for lunch."

He grinned and said, "That's fair."

THIRTY MINUTES LATER, after a nice lunch, we were walking out of *Trello's* into the hustle and bustle of the typical downtown lunch traffic. The sky was clear and the air warm, and on any other day I would have taken a walk through the park to enjoy the weather, but it wasn't any other day. It was a workday and a Monday at that. People were pressed for time to grab a quick bite to eat and return to their desks like the slaves most of us were to our jobs. It made me think about how happy I was that I worked doing something I loved rather than just making money. The money was good too; no doubt about it, but money wasn't everything. I wondered what he thought about working for one's passion or for money, but I didn't want to take the conversation too deep with only a few minutes left until we would be arriving back at work. Our pace as we walked side by side was slow enough that it appeared that we parted the red sea of hurried people as we headed back to the building. Most of the time we were quiet, choosing to only look at each other to communicate, which I liked. Don't get me wrong. I didn't view this as a date or anything exclusive enough to read into it. I saw it as two strangers happening to enjoy lunch together but the occasional thigh or hand brush against his, sent tingling sensations throughout me, sometimes making my breath catch from the intensity of it all. Suddenly I forgot who I was and where the hell I was going. He placed his hand at the small of my back, guiding me to the left so we could turn off on the street where our towering building sat. The contact felt like the fabric of my dress was removed and his palm lay directly against my skin where I actually wanted it. I looked up at him in wonder. Maybe my body was parched for good loving. Maybe that's why his eyes, his voice, even his platonic touch made my body feel so sensitive. *Alive.*

"You are in a daze, huh," he teased as we made it in front of our building and came to a stop. He had no idea how spot-on he was. We were looking at each other in a way that said lunch could potentially be the start of something if either of us made it clear right now. I wouldn't be the first to make a move. I was smarter than that.

"Uh yeah. I guess I don't want to go back. It's the perfect day to do nothing." I looked up to the sky. It was such a beautiful day.

"Nothing and everything, right?"

"Exactly." I looked back at him to find him already staring down at me. Our eyes held. My heart raced.

I licked my lips out of nervousness, I guess, but he watched the movement with unveiled lust.

"I guess we should get going inside."

"You're right. I'm sure you don't want to be seen with me."

"What's that mean?"

"My reputation. Don't want it to stick on you."

"If I cared what other people thought of me, I wouldn't be able to get out of bed." I watched as he smiled like my words pleased him.

"That's practically my mentality."

"Except that the rumors bother you," I pointed out.

"They do but not because they are rumors. They hold truth in them."

"I see."

Hearing his confirmation made me wonder if I could handle getting to know him better if there were ever the opportunity. But I wanted to know him. Like know him beyond what those other women had learned about him.

"As long as you know who you are, it doesn't matter what other people think of you."

"Right now, I can seem to only care about what one person thinks of me."

I knew he was talking about me. "Oh yeah?"

"Yeah. As a matter of fact, let me take down your number. I mean, in case I ever need you to pay for my breakfast again."

We both grinned and stared at each other, neither one of us wanting to drop the connection. Just as he reached into his back pocket and pulled out his phone, someone interrupted.

"Salik. We got to go. Sarah called another meeting." We looked over at a pretty and petite chocolate brown woman. Her manicured hand was on her slim hip, and there was a possessive gleam in her eyes when she looked over at me. I glanced up to find him with a look of confusion on his face, but he didn't seem to want to make a scene, so I helped him out, which I guess was me being the typical too nice Carina.

"It's okay. I'll do my best to be around if you need a few bucks to bail you out," I managed to say even though my heart plummeted.

His smile seemed distracted as if he wanted to say more but decided against it. He nodded instead and walked towards Ms. Chocolate, who flashed her eyes at me as they went inside of the double glass doors. I stood there for a moment trying to collect myself. I stood there just long enough to shake my mind clear of my unofficial date with one of the finest men on earth and then I decided to focus back on the job I was paid to do.

SALIK

"Why would Sarah be calling another meeting, Dom?" We had walked quietly to the elevator, and I followed her on before asking what had me perplexed from the moment she interrupted me getting Carina's number. Sarah calling another meeting was unusual since she was big on scheduling them with her team ahead of time. If she called you in out of the blue, it was usually not a good sign.

Dom stayed silent for a moment and stared at her reflection in the elevator's shiny steel doors. She ran her long red talon-like nails through her silky weave before turning to me and saying slowly like I was a stupid child. "There is no meeting."

"Then what the fuck was that?" I had had it

with her shit today. So much so that I couldn't manage to contain my anger or my language with her. Being nice just didn't seem to matter anymore because she wasn't treating me with the respect I deserved as a single muthafucking man. First the weird vibes and then the ... cock blocking. Not that I was trying to go that far with Carina, at least not really, or not *yet*

"Hey, why the anger?" She had the nerve to ask me.

I just waited for an explanation.

"You said you were done getting involved with women that work here. I was saving you from yourself."

I pulled in a deep breath to try to calm down and avoid yelling but before I released the breath, I knew my deep breathing had not worked.

"I do whatever the fuck I want to do, Dom. Next time stay out of my business. I didn't ask you to be my chaperone."

She was going to say something but thank God for us both, these elevators were prompt about getting us to our floors and the doors opened. I didn't wait for whatever lame excuse she had to give. I was done with Dom. Now I had to figure out how to get another shot at Carina. Serendipity had already happened once. There was no chance it would happen again.

Despite my best intentions on finding a way to connect with Carina, I was busy from the time I got back to my desk to the time I was scheduled to leave and still I couldn't immediately walk out without Sarah stopping me to talk about the project that seemed to never be close to done. Once I assured her that John and I had it under control, I made my way to the elevators. Dom was standing there waiting with a long look on her face. So the fuck what.

Alright, so here is the truth about most men, at least men trying to do right, get it right, and live right. We don't want trouble. At least not beyond the fun kind. Yes, we may deal with multiple women at one time until we've settled down, but even that is about happiness for us. The trouble is a consequence and after doing that too many times for it to remain fun, we typically slow down because what's more important than a whole bunch of fun? Peace. Peace is priceless. Dom was everything else but peace today. I mean, from the moment I saw her in the *real* team meeting, to this moment right here where I was being cornered, she was aggravating me. Even if she meant enough to me for me to want to try and smooth things over with her, it wouldn't be now, not at work. I would need time to think about things and calm down before being forced to have a conversation.

"I saw you talking to Sarah and figured I'd wait for you."

"But why?"

"So that I could apologize."

"No need."

"But isn't there? Aren't you upset with me for ending your conversation with your new friend?" She was practically seething. I would remain cool.

"I'm more upset that you aren't respecting my desire for space honestly."

"I thought we were friends, Salik."

"We *were*. Work friends though. And this is not how you act with a friend from work, Dom."

The hurt in her eyes was apparent, but I hated to say this to myself; I really didn't care. I would give a shit, if Dom and I had been involved beyond one screw. Or if we were the kind of friends that shared everything. But she wasn't my boy Dougie or even Keenan who I met a few years ago when we were both taking courses at CMU. Even though we only saw each other a few times a year now that he moved out to Cali, when we did catch up, we barely left out a detail. I hadn't been like that with Dom.

There was plenty she didn't know and the *only* reason she knew about all the women in the building was because all the women in the building ran their mouths. Not me. A man, a real man, didn't talk.

"Don't do this, Salik?"

I looked around to see if I could find a clue as to why she was really tripping. The only thing I found were a few eyes from my coworkers, and unfortunately those of Sarah. Everyone's attention was trained on us from inside the bullpen area. I'm guessing Dom's agitated voice was causing the stir. And I had to wonder what the fallout would be over this.

"Listen, I don't know what your problem is, but this is too much," I lowered my voice hoping she would do the same, but she looked about ready to blow and I needed to diffuse the situation or my situation at work would go from sex rumors to domestic issues and I'd be fired.

"Look let's talk tomorrow, okay?"

As if on cue, an elevator arrived with a ding, and I was relieved to see her move towards it to get on. I held back though because no matter what, I needed to place some more distance between us. When she stepped into the elevator car and turned, she looked at me to see if I was coming.

"Tomorrow. We'll talk."

She nodded as the doors closed. I don't know how we got to this place, but regardless, I had to part ways with Dom, and it started right here and now.

CARINA

Tossing and turning all night had me as irritated as I had been when I decided that going to bed early would cure my mood. What a joke that had been. Even my yoga instructor felt the tension in my body and kept trying to get me to find my center and breathe the stress out. By time we wrapped up our session, she made recommendations on some herbal tea, chakra unblocking methods, and meditation tools I could use when at home. Honestly, I rolled my eyes when I got in my car, rushed home and got in the shower to do what I was sure would work. Masturbation.

Under the almost scalding spray of water, I cleansed my body first. Once I was sure I took care of the reason I jumped in the shower, I started thinking about Salik as if he were mine. My thoughts fled to what he might do to me if I was willing to be his next notch on his bedpost. In my fantasy, the other notches disappeared, and only *I* remained. It was only me with his lips on mine, his hands in my hair, and his hard dick against my stomach. He knew exactly how to kiss me, exactly how to touch me. His groans were proof that he was enjoying this as much as I was. When his hands reached down to cup my ass, I was ready to have him inside of me. I grabbed his heavy dick and stroked it until he pulled away from my hand.

"Turn around, place your hands on the wall." His voice was scruffy, and it only turned me on more.

I didn't fuss with him, nor did I even take time to consider the dangers of slipping in the shower. Instead, I assumed the position with my palms against the wall and cried out when he thrust inside of me a beat later. He moved inside of me with such intensity that my canal rippled around him as if trying to choke the shit out of his dick. It wasn't long before my body seized, and I exploded all over his ... I mean *my* fingers. Reality came back to me and as it did, my frustration returned. A man that had the ability to make me cum on his imaginary dick while I risked my life in the shower, was a man that should be here with me right now.

I washed off again and exited the shower with disappointment. As great as that orgasm was, it did not replace dick. It did not replace a real live man. There was no earthly cure for my irritation, it seemed. I needed to get into some spiritual place to untangle my emotions because I kept turning the events of the day around in my mind.

I didn't lack for male company but did for that quality stand-by-your-side companionship. That seemed to be most women these days, honestly. We lacked real, honest, true companionship. Not that men were the only problem. Not in my opinion anyway. It just seemed like we all, men and women, were screwed up some kind of way and trying to figure it out or figure out what and whom we really wanted. Years, more like decades, of watching generations of people get married only to end up unhappy, miserable, fighting, and destroying children's lives, had millennials wondering if the happily-ever-after was even something to aspire to have. The "get the bag" mentality had taken over, and younger people seemed more focused on self-development and achievement than romance or life partnership. None of that was wrong either, but it wasn't everything. I wanted the bag, and the man, truthfully. Even still, I put little expectation into the dates I went on and even the sex I sometimes allowed myself to have. When they got up to go before the sun even rose in the sky, I shrugged it off. Staying with me in my home would mean we'd have to have a conversation, and what would we talk about? After you get past the BS and lies, there is usually nothing left. Very few people seemed to like to tell the truth about themselves if they even knew the truth about themselves. That required they be vulnerable and also be open to love.

I tend not to have trouble being open with my feelings. I was the opposite of most in that regard. Maybe it was back to wanting to please people and wanting them happy, but I wanted me happy too. I wanted to love and be loved in return. The challenge was opening up to people and finding they were only there to do more harm than good.

In the short time that I spent with Salik, I felt like he appreciated me being me. I know. I was getting ahead of myself fantasizing about something that really wasn't even there. From the looks of things, he wasn't done messing with people in the building. Spewing all that talk about his reputation, and feeling like it was following him everywhere, was all just conversation. I had to wonder if anything that we talked about, if anything that I felt when we were connecting was actually real.

So yeah, during yoga and after my shower, and even after drinking my cup of chamomile tea, I still had trouble relaxing and sleeping. I ended up searching social media to see if I could find him and find out a little about him like a crazy stalker. I located him on Facebook and Instagram. His Facebook was set to private and the public posts that were there, dated years back, revealed very little about him. But his Instagram was public. I scrolled through mostly posts of him with his siblings and some at a barbershop where he was doing some computer repair work. No women, not partying, nothing that would paint him in a doggish light. I was confused. Who was the man I had lunch with? Sinner or saint? There would be no answers now that our vibe was killed, so I went to sleep without solving the riddle.

For that reason, I walked into work the following morning a grumpy woman. I made my way over to the kiosk, desperately hoping that I wouldn't run into him this time. I had opened up my feelings, maybe not even feelings, maybe it was just the possibility of having any feelings to share that I allowed myself, and I didn't need to do that again today. Lesson learned. But when I stepped to the counter to place my order this time, not forgetting the breakfast sandwich, Tony gave me a smile.

"What's with you today?"

"Oh, nothin'."

I twisted my lips and inspected him. "How's Michelle and the kids?" Tony and his wife seemed to have a new baby every year so maybe that was it, is what I was thinking.

"They're fine. Now stop trying to read me. Here's your drink and sandwich. " He slid my bag and cup across the counter to me and I reluctantly picked it up as I felt the line starting to form behind me.

"But I haven't even paid you yet."

"And? Get to work and we'll talk tomorrow when you step in the doors."

I grumbled but had to acquiesce because I would be late trying to fool around with him. Late and beat up, based on the irritated looks on the faces of two of my coworkers waiting for me to get out the way so they could place their orders. I gave them a sheepish smile and hurried to the escalator leading up to the elevators.

CARINA

I arrived at work most days before the rush, so it was still quiet in the bullpen. Tracey's desk was still empty with no sign that she was in, which was good because I still needed time to come to peace with the wave of emotions of yesterday. I figured it was best just to let it go rather than reflect which would only make me remember how for about one full hour, I was caught up in a man who had no intention of doing more than having sex with me and discarding me like everyone else had sex with at KIB. And then I pulled my sandwich out of the bag and a paper, slipped out with it. Written in neat handwriting, it said:

. . .

Carina-

I HOPE I'm spelling it right.

I wanted to apologize first for not getting the chance to end our non-date the right way. Being called off for a meeting was unexpected. But, and I mean this, I would like to have another non-date. Just us somewhere. I'll understand if you're against that, but if you're good with it, call or text me.

Salik 555-412-1212

I LOOKED DOWN at the white-lined paper note for a while as if more words would appear or change and would have continued if not for Tracey clearing her throat as she stepped over to my desk. I was beginning to wonder if Tracey only got paid to be cute here because lately, she was at my desk more than her own.

"What's that?"

I quickly folded the small paper up and slid it

under my phone. "Nothing. Just a list of things I need to grab after work."

"Mmmmhmmm, go on ahead and hide your secrets but trust me they won't be secrets for long if Dominique has anything to do with it."

I was confused which is why I asked her, "Who's Dominique?"

"Apparently, you two met when you were coming back from lunch with Salik. The man you aren't interested in …remember?" Did I mention that Tracey knows everyone and everything in this building?

"It was no big deal."

"Tell that to Dominique who is telling everyone that you and Salik were practically falling all over each other in front of the building.

"She a damn lie."

"Oh I know and I said as much, but who knows how many other people she said this to. So now you are on the list of Salik's victims."

"Uggggghhhhh, why?"

She shrugged.

"People love to talk. And when there's nothing to talk about, they find something to talk about. Give it a minute to die down."

I slumped in my chair and wished I could leave

from work already and I hadn't even had my breakfast yet. That's how early it still was.

"It's been one day of contact with a man I had never met before and now there are gossips being written about me. I never even met this Dominique until yesterday. But she seemed to have a thing for Salik."

"I think so too and quiet as it's kept, it seems like it was definitely one-sided."

That got my interest.

"How do you know?"

She smiled as if she figured out I was more interested in Salik than I wanted to put on. And I was.

"Call it a hunch. But Imma say this and then be done with it. Tread carefully. Not because of Dominique or any of these bitches here. But because your heart deserves the very best. Have fun, but don't get tangled up in it."

"When did you become so wise?" I watched as her eyes grew somber.

"Life taught me a lot of things, usually by lobbing blows at me."

"I hear you."

"No, you don't. I hope you never do either."

Before I could ask her more, she got up from my spare chair and went to her corner of the universe. I knew the time for that discussion had ended —that she had let me as far in as she would want me to be.

I got to work on my laptop and took bites of my sandwich and sips of my coffee sporadically, thinking about the rumors that I was now a part of and of Dominique. If what Tracey said was true, yesterday's interruption was about more than a team meeting. Dom was trying to keep Salik from seeing anyone else. I wasn't into games, especially ones that reeked of high school mean girl BS. Getting involved with him even for just sex would mean drama, but hadn't I expressed just how boring my life had been?

I pulled out his note and without giving it too much more thought, plugged his number into my contacts and pressed "send message".

ME: I'm down.
    -Carina

I HURRIED to put my phone away just so that I didn't obsess about his response or how long it would take to even get a response, but it vibrated before I could slide it into my purse.

. . .

Salik: You just made my day. Real talk.

So guess what? He and I texted all day. I barely got any work done which was okay because I had been so far ahead on everything. I could afford to have a day where I horsed around.

Salik: When's the last time you actually went to a concert?
 Me: Ages ago.
 Salik: What's ages?
 Me: Maybe five years.
 Salik: Who did you see?
 Me: It was a Jill Scott concert.
 Salik: I bet it was nice.
 Me: It was very nice. Chrisette Michelle opened it.
 Salik: Oh well, that mighta been way longer than 5 years ago. 12
 Me: Haha … but you're probably right. 12
 Salik: I know that I am.
 Me: Whatever.

. . .

It was quiet for a few moments with no sign that he was typing a response. That was the only thing about texting; you could never know where the conversation had shifted to. Whether you offended someone or they just got busy or disinterested in talking anymore. They just disappear unless they tell you they have to go.

I waited a few extra minutes for him to come back and when he didn't, I focused back on the job that paid me. An hour passed, and I realized it was time to close up shop. My coworkers were already heading to the elevators. I just had a few more system updates to review before I could go. Ready now, I grabbed my bag and headed out. It was practically a ghost town in the hallway. When I got on the elevator, I finally allowed myself to smile about my day with Salik. And by day, I meant us texting. I enjoyed him. I learned he was one of three children like me, but he was the baby. When I told him he was a spoiled brat, he sent a baby emoji rather than deny it. His mom raised him and his siblings solo, so they did a lot to help her now that they were grown. It was clear even through typed out words, that his mom meant the world to him and he'd do anything for her. Which only made me think about how much I missed my Papa. He died of a heart attack a year ago and the wound still felt fresh some days. For my mom, it was every day of missing my father and knowing he would never come back. He had been the love of our lives, and truthfully, watching them love each other the way they did, made me want love just like it.

The ding of the elevator as I arrived on the ground floor broke me from my thoughts of my parents and love. But when I stepped out into the lobby, I found a surprise. He stood there as if he were waiting for me, leaning against the security desk, casually. His pale blue shirt under his camel sports jacket looked crinkled from the rigors of the long day, and despite that, he looked perfect.

I took a few steps in his direction and watched him straighten up to approach me. The security guard that I would nod at most evenings gave us both a soft smile before minding his business.

"I was wondering if you'd show up?"

"You've been waiting a long time?"

"Just an hour."

"Goodness, that's a long time."

He shrugged. He didn't seem bothered by the wait, and I tried not to think about how much that pleased me. That he was willing to wait as long as necessary and with patience.

"It was worth it. Besides, waiting gave me time to handle some business and chat with Chuck over there." I looked over there at Chuck who was pretending not to be watching us. I didn't want to think about how many women left this building with Salik under Chuck's watch.

I cleared my throat. "Was there something you wanted to say to me that you couldn't say in text?"

He smiled and moved in a few more steps. His cologne was subtle but still strong enough to pull me into him like he was wearing a pheromone and I was completely at his whim because of it. When he was only one small step away, he stopped. I looked up at him and felt dizzy. Like seriously dizzy. Like if he asked for anything from me, anything at all, I would give it to him. No questions asked.

"Only that Lalah Hathaway will be in town this weekend. I got us tickets. I mean, you mentioned loving her voice but not seeing her live in concert. Would you want to go ... with me?

My heart thumped a familiar beat. I suppose it was the beat one felt when someone you are interested in does all the right things, says all the right things, and you have a choice whether to believe in it or flee. Richie never was considerate of my desires and yet I had sex with him with no promise of anything in return, and here Salik was considerate, offering me a good time, and I was almost positive I'd get an orgasm out of it even if I lied to myself and said sex would not be on the menu after the concert.

"I'd love to go."

He smiled like it was the thing he needed to hear to have some sort of peace this day.

Salik walked me to my car, made sure I got off safely and then sent me a text an hour later. I was sipping some tea and re-watching season three of Insecure to prepare for the new season when my phone chimed.

SALIK: You made my day.

Me: I'm sure you have no problem getting women to do whatever you ask them.

IT TOOK a few minutes before he responded.

SALIK: I actually like you which is why I need to say this.

I'm hoping you can put all the gossip, true or not, aside and see me for who I am.

Me: I can. I will.

Salik: Good. Because I'm looking forward to taking you out, having a good time, and seeing what comes next if there's a next for us.

I didn't tell him this, but I was hoping there would be.

SALIK

Carina agreeing to go out with me made my stressful day a lot better. What she didn't know, and I had no plans on telling her, was that there had been a lot of drama in my day stemming from our one innocent lunch. When I arrived at work, it was to find hostile stares coming at me from Dom. Even though she gave me space, I knew she really wanted to be all in my ear arguing over Carina. Let me say this now because I had to remind myself of this earlier. As much as I was digging Carina, it wasn't that deep for me to be losing my job over her. She was fine as fuck, and I enjoyed our lunch, her laughter, the way her eyes softened when she gazed at me from across the table yesterday, and that was something I don't even think she was aware of. With that said, it wasn't at a level where I was ready to fight for her. No. The real problem I had with Dom was how what I wanted to do was being fucked with by someone that I have not, nor would *ever*, be involved with.

So, I avoided Dom and ignored her heated looks, but I couldn't avoid my boss, who wanted to "see me for a chat" later that morning. This was that unexpected meeting I mentioned earlier. The one that never meant anything good. I had been in the middle of texting Carina, mind you when I got pulled in to see Sarah but was surprised to find the head honcho himself, seated in the room as well. I rarely, if ever, saw the man that gave me this opportunity to work here. Khalil Berry, though hands-on when it came to the job, was not nearly as involved in the day-to-day as he had once been or at least that's what I had heard. These days he split his time meeting with department heads and being with his family. Having seen a picture of both his gorgeous wife, Zola, and their son, Zachery, it made complete sense to me that he would opt to spend most of his time in the country, or in their penthouse, with them.

Sarah pointed to the chair across from her desk for me to take a seat. I looked to Khalil, whose expression gave nothing away, as I sat down and wondered what his role was in this meeting.

Sarah fed my curiosity when she offered, "Mr. Berry and I were meeting about something else entirely when I told him I would be meeting with you today. He asked to stay, Salik."

Khalil gave me a slight nod but remained quiet as I gulped. It felt like this was my last meeting with Sarah. All the times I dreaded one on ones with my boss came to mind. I would do anything to have one of those back. Having the CEO seated in here, applied serious pressure but also made it clear to me that my time had run out all because of Dom.

"I wanted to touch base about yesterday, Salik."

"It won't happen again." I hurried to say.

Sarah took a deep breath and looked over to Mr. Berry before giving me a somber look. "Salik, it's bigger than it not happening again. There were a lot of people that saw the exchange and Dominique has said to me that you were hurtful when she tried to settle whatever the dispute was between you."

Now it was I who looked over to Khalil who still remained silent. Despite his silence, it was still clear to me who called the shots around here. It wasn't just his expensive clothes and designer glasses; it was his presence that said this was his space, his house. I was only a visitor. I hoped to one day be in that position of power, but because of Dominique that wouldn't happen, and I hadn't even told my side yet.

"Sarah, there was no dispute. She was angry I went to lunch with someone and that someone wasn't her."

Sarah looked over at Khalil who had a small smile on his face. Sarah looked back at me.

"Are you and Dominique in a relationship? Not that I have a right to know, Salik, just to be clear. She does not report up to you and there's no policy against it otherwise. I'm just trying to get a better picture of what took place."

"No, I thought we were friends."

I refrained from saying more. It was important to me to set boundaries in this conversation. Dominique's behavior put me in an awkward situation, but I was determined to try and get out of it by moving on with my life. Hearing that she had gone to Sarah, and who knows who else and lied about what really happened made it clear to me that I didn't need to settle anything with Dom. I was truly finished.

"At this point, it's her word against yours, and I have no reason to take either side, not yet. Because the exchange was brief and Dominique hasn't reported feeling harassed, I'm going to let you off with a verbal warning. But Salik, you have a promising future here. I really hate to see this escalate, and we have to come back here. It won't be a verbal warning at that time. Do you understand?"

"I do."

"Good."

Finally Khalil decided to speak up. "Sarah, please give me a moment to talk to Salik."

Sarah gave me one of those smiles that she did what she could, but it was above her now before she left her *own* office quietly. This was when Mr. Berry stood.

"You're disappointed," I said before he even could. I'd seen the look he had in his eyes plenty of times before. My mom looked at my siblings and me the same way right before she whooped our asses.

He leaned back against Sarah's desk in front of me and crossed his legs. "What gave you that idea?"

"It's written all over your face."

"I've been told I have a pretty good poker face, so are you sure the disappointment is from me? Maybe it's from inside of you, Salik."

I gave him a nervous laugh and wondered when he had time to become a shrink too.

"See, I've been where you are," he said.

I highly doubted that. "In what way?"

He shrugged. "My mess catching up with me."

"How'd you get out of it?"

"Being honest with myself first and then being apologetic. Honesty is the work for guys like us."

"Like us?" I tilted my head and stared at him like he was crazy. How was I like him?

"Yep. Two black men. Two handsome black men that women love." He was unfazed by my expression.

"Oh." He had a point, but I also knew that those were the only things we had in common.

"Being rich isn't everything you know."

I looked at him. I was shocked at him voicing something that had been nagging me. He had it all. How could he sit here and judge me?

"I see how you look at me—I saw it the first time you saw me in the barbershop. Like I got it all, and it's because I'm *The* Khalil Berry that I have it all. But brotha let me tell you, when I walk in the door every day, I'm nothing but a man, a black man, mortal in some places, a god in others. Me all the time. Most of all, I just want my wife, Zola, to make it all worth it. She always does. This thing that I built here in this building came from my passion, but everything at home came from love."

That was some deep shit. I sat back.

"So, what I'm about to say comes from my passion, but also from my love for the most beautiful women in the world, black women. You got to be honest with yourself. And you must respect them. No more of this using your dick to feel like a man in KIB."

I felt scolded but rightfully so. Even though I had given up the exploits, I had done a lot of damage here in this building and trying to defend that because I had stopped doing it some months ago, seemed silly.

"I'm through with it, Mr. Berry."

"Call me Khalil.

"I'm done, Khalil. For real. I stopped months ago but Dominique, I thought understood what we had was casual and temporary. It doesn't excuse my behavior, however, so I'm with you. I agree. It's wrong.

He nodded.

"I don't want to see you mess up an opportunity here, Salik. Part of the reason I started this company was to give my people a chance in a way that we don't often get."

"And I admire that and don't want to ruin it."

"Good. Now before I head out ... the one you took to lunch. She someone special?"

The smile on his face told me he knew the answer.

"I think so; it's too soon to know for sure. Problem is, she works here."

He lifted a shoulder. "If she's special go for it but treat her like who she is. Feel me?

"I feel you."

WE CHATTED a few more minutes before he allowed me to get back to work. I appreciated the talk with him, one that he definitely did not have to take the time with me to have , just to get me to see myself from a different angle. Being honest with myself meant being honest about how my actions hurt women. Maybe I was upfront with them all, but after the first woman, and maybe even the second, I should have known that none of them could handle whatever it was I was on. I didn't need to keep pulling them in and then spitting them out. That was God's honest truth.

Dominique was a different matter for me altogether, however. I was this close to losing my job over some bullshit she was up to. It was then that I understood why some unstable types lost their sanity at work. Most people spent most of their time at their place of employment. There were a ton of interpersonal relationships at play when you walked in the front doors and punched in. With your coworkers, your supervisors, everyone. Sometimes that shit went bad, and yet you were expected to grin and bear it like nothing was wrong. And let's not even discuss if you have other problems at home.

As I got back to working through some encryptions to ready a panel for John to take over, I had to think about whether I wanted to keep going with Carina after my talk with Khalil. She was special; even a blind man could see that about her, but for a moment I worried whether I would fuck it up with her and everything would come crumbling down. But then I thought about how Khalil's face lit up when he talked about his wife. No, I wasn't thinking about marriage, not by any means, but having someone light up my life like that was something I never had. Carina could be the one, but I had to first get to know her.

A few minutes later, I started thinking about date ideas and remembered she was into neo-soul music. When I googled "concerts near me", Lalah Hathaway popped up. Serendipity came to mind again. What were the chances that one of Carina's favorite artists would be in town in a few days and I could secure front-row seats? The chances were slim to none, so I didn't even think twice about it. I hurried to secure the tickets and hoped like hell she'd say yes to going.

When she arrived in the lobby off the elevator, I knew my day had been worth it and she hadn't even agreed to go. She may have gone undetected for years in this building but there was no way I could ever miss her now. She was the star here. Her skin was vibrant, her hair shiny, lustrous, healthy. Her lashes were so long they touched her cheek when she closed her eyes long enough. Her lips were pouty and soft. She was stunning. Before she even looked up, I decided I wanted to do her better than I did the others. Not that I was unkind to anyone else, but seriously, I wanted to see if Carina and I could have a shot. But, even as the thoughts entered my mind, I was shaking my head. *Salik, you are moving too fast. You don't even know the girl.*

But I didn't need to know her to know I wanted her more than just to screw her. So when she agreed to go out with me, I was determined to make it one of her best dates.

CARINA

The entire week at work seemed to move at a snail's pace and I knew it was because I was looking forward to my date with Salik, whom I had been texting all week. In addition, we'd been to lunch on both Wednesday and Thursday at Trello's. When As Todd served us our food with a smile, I asked Salik if he was buttering me up for our date; he looked at me so seriously that my smile was wiped off my face as he rumbled out, "Nah, this is what a man does when he's interested, and I'm very interested." *Well okay.*

I had no doubt that he was interested. His eyes, his voice, and his constant communication with me said that he was more than interested, but I wondered for how long. One of the hardest things to do for a single person, a single woman in particular, on the precipice of maybe finding a good thing with someone, is slowing down the mental talk where we weigh all the possibilities and think about the future before the present even has a chance to take off. I knew that it was too soon to hope that Salik would or could be someone I could spend some real time with and enjoy it and yet that's exactly what I was doing. Moving too fast even in my mind. But … and this is me being completely transparent with myself… no one stayed. I mean no one that *I* wanted to stay, anyway. It would be nice to have someone want me as much as I wanted them and show me that by staying past that night and into the next.

It also didn't help that my manager, Sharise seemed to be on my tail more than usual. She even called me into see her right as I was packing up to leave and go home. When I knocked on the door to her small corner office, she asked me to have a seat before spending another five minutes tapping around on her computer. I spent the time looking around at her office space. No pictures of family, no plants or flowers. Everything was functional as if she'd be ready to walk out a of there at moment's notice without a box if asked to. Me, on the other hand, had pictures of my parents, sister and brother, me and my girl Desi who was abroad studying art. I had all kinds of junk cluttering my desk and cubicle walls to remind me that work wasn't everything. I had to wonder if for Sharise, work was in fact everything.

When she finally finished with whatever she was doing, she glanced at me hard.

"I wanted to check in to see where you were on your quality checks before the weekend."

I avoided tilting my head at her. "Well, I'm on schedule, if that's what you're asking."

"I just need to make sure that you can handle the workload that's been assigned. Especially since you put in for that promotion."

I detected a tinge of something in her voice. Jealousy, aggravation, something. Where was this coming from?

"I asked you if you were supportive of me making that move, Sharise. Has something changed?"

This is when she leaned forward and placed her hands together in front of her on her desk like she was the principal and I'd just been sent to her office.

"No, nothing has changed but the job requires a higher level of commitment. I wanted to make sure you were up to the task.

"I believe I am. Pretty sure of it." My words came

out slowly as I tried to wrap my brain around this meeting with her.

"Good, good. That's it, Carina."

I took my time moving out of the chair and watched her just long enough for her to go back to messing around on her computer. Something was up with Sharise and to be honest, I didn't feel like figuring out just what it was because my nerves were wound up about my date with Salik.

I did manage to quiet the chatter in my mind the remainder of the week. Maybe it was a talk with my sister who seemed to go from one failed relationship to the next. When she called me between making her rounds to see what I had been up to, I shared that I was going on a date.

"Not with Richie?" She pictured her nose scrunched up as if she were disgusted.

I chuckled. "No, not Richie, though you got a lot of nerve. Wasn't it you that encouraged me to give Richie a chance?"

She laughed into the phone. "Yeah but that was before you told me he was selfish in bed." *And had a little dick* but I would have never shared that.

"Mmmmhmmm. Well no, not Richie. His name is Salik."

"Sexy name, Sis."

"Sexy man, Sis."

I could hear a voice over the hospital intercom's system. They were calling a code.

"You got to go?"

"No, I'm not on the code team right now. We have a few more minutes."

I smiled. Between her hospital schedule and Yusef living in Texas now, it wasn't often that I got to be around my brother and sister. Talking to Tori was a treat.

"So, tell me about this man you're going out with. I'll live vicariously through you."

I shook my head and told her everything from top to bottom.

"Are you worried you'll get played?'

"Definitely."

"And you're going out with him anyway?"

"Yeah, because why not? I can stop things before they go too far."

"Or you get so caught up you forget to stop it before it goes too far."

"That's entirely possible."

"Yep. But I say you're doing the right thing and going for it. You only live once."

"Wow."

"Not what you were expecting me to say huh?"

"No, not at all, Tori."

She was quiet for a moment as if reflecting.

"Well let's just say that someone needs to give mommy some grand babies and I probably ruined my chances at that."

"Don't say that. You should never give up hope on love."

"You would say that. You're the sweetest of three of us. I'm not like you though. Men have always come last in my life. To everything. Not just this job either. Don't make that mistake. Live, take chances and if you get hurt, you heal. But … if you find love, embrace it."

When Friday arrived, I was more than ready to go out with Salik. I took a half-day off, much to Sharise's chagrin, and treated myself to a spa retreat. I was waxed, tweezed, massaged, and my face soothed with a facial. When I got home, I showered and slathered on some body oil that had my skin soft and glowing. I pulled out the black dress I got on sale from Fashion Nova. The material was a little slinky and plunged down in the front to show off my cleavage. The hem of the dress hit me at mid-thigh so in my black strappy heels, my legs looked fantastic. My legs were one of the parts of my body that I didn't want to be changed by my yoga work. They were long, curvy, sexy and when I wore heels, they helped to emphasize my entire shape.

I spent some more time getting myself together while I played some Maxwell to bring me into the mood I wanted to have with Salik. I wanted to feel calm, sexy and confident. I wanted to be ready for whatever. I tidied up my bedroom to get rid of any sign of the clothes I had tossed on the bed, or the shoes I went back and forth on before settling on these. Just as I made it out into my living room, my doorbell rang. Taking a deep breath I moved towards the door, paused and said a little prayer.

Please let this be the start of something different and new.

It was simple really. Nothing heavy was placed on him to meet or exceed an expectation he couldn't rise to. It was just a prayer for something that I'd never had before. I trusted the Universe to give me something my heart desired. He took one look at me when I opened the door and said, "Damn, Carina. You look so damn good."

He did too. A dark tweed sports coat over a cream button up top left open at his broad neck, dark blue jeans that hung relaxed over soft brown leather loafers. Fresh haircut faded into a low cut fro, lips looking soft and ready for my lips and body. It took everything in me to walk out my front door rather than pull him inside so he could show me he meant how good he thought I looked. Instead, I chose the date, the music, and the fun with Salik. I allowed him to lead me to his silver Range Rover and help me in and enjoyed smelling his cologne and imaging running my nose up his neck before gently biting his ear.

Three hours later, after he helped me out of his truck, we were walking hand in hand to the front door of my condo. To say this date was more perfect than any others I had before it, would be an understatement. I also wouldn't be able to explain why it was perfect, only that from the moment we started our experience … you know what …. that's it. It was an *experience*. He treated me like I was someone special, and the energy coming off him in waves told me he really liked me. Then when we went through security at the Byham Theater to be shown our seats and I found out he got us front row seats to see Lalah Hathaway! I was outdone. The opening act was Rashaad, who I learned through Salik was related to Khalil Berry. Rashaad was the life partner or maybe husband of Khalil's niece Zoe. Well anyway, he had this so sexy, dope vibe about him that made me think he needed to be the main show to be honest.

He played his guitar in such a way that it sounded like *it* was singing before he even belted out the first notes. For his second and last number, he actually brought out his wife, Zoe, who swayed in front of him as he stood and looked down at her. It was clear to anyone looking on that he loved his woman. At the end of the song titled *Hazel*, he kissed her slowly. The crowd ooh'd and aww'd and then clapped when the two of them came up for air.

Salik looked down at me, and it felt like everyone and everything around us was disappearing. His eyes said he wanted to do the same to me as Rashaad had done to his wife, but that he was unsure if it was too soon. It wasn't. My heels brought me closer to his height, but I still had to lean upon my toes a little to meet his lips. His grasp around my waist tightened as he accepted my kiss and deepened it with a swirl of his tongue around mine. Our lips moved around each other as our breaths pulled from each other, allowing us to keep our connection. The kiss stirred so much passion inside of me that the warmth I felt between my thighs was a sign of the dew he was pulling from my body without even manipulating it yet. I wanted him too though. I wanted him to have everything. I wanted him to taste me and feel me. Tonight.

Before long, the band for Lalah took over the stage and began testing out their instruments while we still kissed. We couldn't seem to pull away from the temptation to connect, taking quick but passionate snatches of kisses from each other before going full on into a mesmerizing tangle of tongues and lips. We didn't worry what anyone else thought because weren't dates for talking, kissing, and making out? However, the clickety-clack bang-bang of the drums had us pulling apart. My skin felt hot, my lips felt swollen, my head was in the clouds. *I want this man right now*, I thought.

CARINA

When we entered my place, nerves started building inside of me. Anticipation could do that to a girl on the brink of what was sure to be some bomb ass dick. The confidence I had earlier took a backseat, as he paced around my living room, looking at photos and artwork nailed to my walls. I thought about how I wanted him to nail my walls but didn't want to be overly aggressive about it.

Instead, I asked. "Would you like anything to drink?" He turned away from the framed Basquiat print and looked at me.

"Nah. Water can wait." I watched as he removed his jacket and placed it on my oversized chair before training his eyes back on me.

I gulped. The invitation back to my place wasn't exactly explicit consent, but if we were real with each other, it was what I wanted, and he knew it. At this point he was just waiting for me to make it clear that he could make a move before he touched me.

"What do you want … at least right now?"

"I think you know. Just say the word and we can both get what we want, Carina."

"I want you, Salik. Touch me please." My words were clear enough.

The lighting was too dim to be sure, but it looked as if his eyes closed on a prayer for a moment before he moved towards me and pulled me closer to him. His large hands cupped my face and brought me into his kiss. I ran my hands up and down his large biceps wishing his shirt was already gone. I reached around him and held onto his broad back feeling the strength of his passion brimming beneath his gentle touch. Our kiss deepened and we moved our heads side to side as we tongued each other down in my living room. Finally, he pulled away and asked me where my bedroom was. I took his hand and led him to my room around the corner and down the hall, our steps echoing against the walls as our steps hit my hardwood floors. When we arrived inside of my room, he looked around only long enough to figure out the setup before pulling me in his arms again. I was dizzy with passion, lust, and under his command but needed to find a way to participate in my own experience. This time I pulled away from his tempting lips and slipped out of my heels before reaching down to pull my dress slowly up my body and over my head.

"Fuck." His head moved side to side as if in disbelief when I stood in front of him in my black strapless bra and black thongs.

"Turn around, Carina," he whispered to me, and I immediately thought of my shower fantasy while I complied.

"Your body is so fucking beautiful. So lush." His hand reached out and touched me. First at my shoulder and then came down my arm, around to my side and down to my hip where he squeezed my curves. He treated each roll and valley like it was divine and he intended to worship me. Just then, I heard him behind me, beginning to remove his clothing and not wanting to miss the spectacular sight of him undressing, I turned to watch. The grin on his face said he wouldn't get on me for turning around before he demanded it, but this wasn't *Simon Says* anyway. I wanted to see every bit of him as he was seeing of me. When his shirt lay in a pile near his feet, I realized his body was more magnificent than I could imagine.

I held my breath when he reached for his leather belt and began to undo it. He made quick work of removing his pants and slipping out of his loafers and kicking them aside. He reached down to grab his Gucci wallet out of his back pocket before placing it on my nightstand. Then he stood in front of me in his boxers. I wanted to see the rest because what I could see was the body of a god. Ripped, brown chocolate goodness. His thighs were cut, strong and long, making me want to ride him fast and hard. As if he read my mind, he reached out for me, and I went to him wondering when I would see the rest of what I desired. He distracted me with his kisses again, however, his hands moved around my back, my waist, and my hips before he began squeezing each half of my cheeks together. The friction of the movement reverberated to my sensitive clit that was already so engorged. It puckered out from where it usually rested between my fat lips, wanting his attention, hoping he would give it to her. She's needed it for a long time. He must have known it too because very slowly he helped me out of my bra. He lifted the weight of my breasts in his large palms and brought each one to his lips, taking turns to suck my nipples. They were hard, damp from his wet mouth and begging for more when he pulled away.

I whimpered. He responded by going back to them first with his thumbs as he flicked the tips and twirled them, then with his lips as he teased pulled them into his mouth. The suction, the intensity of it all, had me practically begging for him to pull out his dick.

"I need you ..." If only he would stop playing and give me what I wanted most.

"You'll have me," he promised, kissing my lips again.

If I thought he would take me out of my misery and make his way inside of me, I was sadly mistaken. Instead, he very deliberately, pulled my thong down from around my hips and between my thighs until it slid to the floor. His hand cupped my mound and he bit his lip when he found all the wetness waiting for him.

"It's all down your thighs, Carina. Damn." He sounded so pleased and all I could manage to do was moan out as he began to ply my engorged bud with his finger.

Finally, he helped me into my bed and had me spread out on top of my comforter. Still in his boxers, he leaned over me and started at my lips again. Kissing them, then sucking on my neck, enflaming me to the point I felt ready to combust. Then his mouth was on my breasts, pushing them together and sucking both nipples at the same time until I begged him to, "Please fuck me."

His soft chuckle was his only response as he moved down my body, landing kisses against my soft midsection and then my thighs. He moved them apart and pushed them back to my chest and before I could even wonder about what would happen next, he was sucking me deliciously. The sounds of his sucking, his licking, but most of all, his enjoyment in tasting me, set me on fire. I couldn't contain my moans of pleasure or keep myself from reaching for his head and holding him to me as he feasted. He praised me with the action by groaning into my flesh. His finger came to rest at my opening, applying pressure there. I wanted it in me. I needed something, just anything to give me something to hold on to. He pressed and entered my folds with his finger and moved his thick digit in and out and he swirled around my clit. I shattered and screamed this man's name.

That must have been what he was waiting for because as I panted and tried to collect myself, he stood up and pulled his black boxer briefs down.

Okay, damn! Salik had a monster dick and I had to wonder for one tiny moment if I could handle him. After having something less than mediocre with Richie the past few months, my body might have shrunk up. But I would not voice my doubts, nah. I just leaned up on my elbows and watched as he removed a magnum condom from the wrapper and then unrolled it to cover his pipe, I mean dick. I swallowed hard as he turned to me. He got on the bed with me, and I settled back onto the bed and opened my legs as he slid up my body. When he kissed me the next moment, my worries disappeared. His hands moved beneath my ass and tilted my hips for what came next.

He slid in slowly, allowing me to get used to the size of him, thank God. But despite my inner worry, my body welcomed his with no problem. I mean I felt him, all of him, but it felt good to be filled up and the slow winding movements from his hips, only increased the pleasure. I clutched his back and his ass at various times just to keep a hold of myself because my body wasn't used to feeling so much pleasure all over. I didn't know what to do with that. But when he sucked on my lip and started to give me those short, punctuated taps, I lost myself. There was no control.

"Fuckkkkk, Salik."

"Yeah, baby. What is it?"

"Oh damn."

"I know."

I don't know what he knew, but I knew I was cumming on his dick and screaming like a banshee while he just kept drilling like there was oil inside of me. I suppose there was because moments later, Salik had me flip over on my stomach. I called myself popping it back on him to give it better than I got it, but dammit, his dick made me lose my mind. Each thrust sent me to outer space, it seemed. I heard him say, "Shit, baby" like I was doing something. I had no idea what it could have been because he was in complete control. He mastered me on night one. Later I would learn that I had squirted on the man's chest. But at this moment, all I knew was that Salik was going to have me in every position manageable with no sign of finishing himself. Not until I asked to get on top. He allowed me to slide down on top of him and this is where I gave him a little show. I teased my breasts for him while rocking my hips back and forth and round and round. Then I started giving him a hard ride, lifting and falling on his hard wood so good that I was worried I would cum again before he did. Our eyes connected as I worked, and I reached down to grab his hands to place them against my bouncing breasts. He caressed them as I rode his length swiftly, expertly. I could feel his body tensing beneath mine which was good because not only was I growing tired, but my body was ready for another release. I reached behind me with one hand and massaged his balls slick with my wetness and that was it. He started to shake and finally I allowed myself to succumb to what I held back. I screamed out again and collapsed on Salik's heaving chest. He held me as our breathing slowed. He held me even after we took a shower to clean off the sweat and the cum, and when we got back in bed, under the covers this time, he held me until I fell asleep.

In the morning, I woke up to find him not in bed with me. I lied to myself about why my chest hurt where my heart was beating. I told myself that I had a good time, the best time so I shouldn't be hurt that he left. I told myself all of this as I tried to accept that it was what it was, and nothing more. But I heard a noise coming from what sounded like my kitchen, and I grabbed my robe off the hook on my bedroom door. When I entered the kitchen, it was to find a naked Salik making me coffee.

"You need help?" He turned to the sound of my voice and eyed me in blue silk robe with unveiled lust. I, however, tried to avoid the sight of his heavy penis in the daylight. I was too shocked at his presence to process two things at once. *He was still here?*

"Just looking for your mugs." I took measured steps over to the cabinet on the opposite side of the kitchen and reached up to grab two before looking back at him.

"You made me coffee?" I could smell the aroma and it smelled heavenly, almost as good as my own.

"Yeah, but I don't need a mug," he said, looking at the two I sat down on the counter. "I don't drink the stuff, but I figured since you had some, you drank it."

"I do."

We stared at each other, and I could feel that he wanted me again and I for damn sure wanted him again. Especially now that I knew he was different. For once a man stayed.

SALIK

I had never in my life made coffee for a woman before I made it for Carina. I had never even seen it being made growing up. Not to say my mother didn't drink it—she did. It was the only thing that helped her work her two or three jobs to feed me and my brothers, Isaiah and Kareem. She had one of those carafe type devices that doled out multiple cups of brew for her, so yeah, I've been around it. It was just that I was a boy that stayed out of the kitchen. I left that to my mom and her sisters, and only occasionally dipped in to lick the icing bowl, or to hear a little gossip to report back to my brothers. Coffee making was definitely not a skill I obtained over the years either. But when I opened my eyes this morning, with my body flush against Carina's soft curves, I knew I would make sure she woke up to something, anything. My black ass couldn't cook worth a damn, so coffee seemed like the logical choice when I couldn't find anything else to impress her with. And when she entered the kitchen looking soft and tousled, I knew I wanted to impress her with more than coffee. She didn't say it, but I caught a glimpse of relief in seeing that I was still around when she woke up. It made me think about how many women's homes I left out of in the middle of the night or early in the morning before they woke up to ask me to stay. I always made sure I secured their place when I left, but I didn't secure their feelings. Sure, some if not most of them, were expecting me to be gone. Didn't mean that it didn't hurt that I had actually left. Carina was likely a woman that was victim of the same behavior. She didn't deserve that. She deserved someone to stay, and I was only happy it was me that chose to stay. I got to put in the time and effort to show her I was for real.

I didn't have a man in my life to show me what being a man really was about. I had to piece together what I learned from my mother, from the streets, from school, from Marlon, and from breaking hearts. I'm not making any excuses about how I did or didn't treat women. Only that outside of my young puppy love, I didn't know how to take care of the most important part of a woman's entirety: her heart. The placed that housed her spirit. Breaking a woman's heart also killed her spirit. I was starting to understand that a little more. Just in time to do better with Carina.

Our date last night was dope. The music and the vibe were perfect for us getting to know each other. There wasn't much talking, of course, but talking isn't the only way to get to know someone. The way she moved with grace, the way she smelled, how soft her hair felt when it brushed against my face when as I would lean in to tell her something over the music. Even how she embraced my touch while we were at the concert, all of that was confirmation for me that she and I were vibing heavy, and immediately I wanted to give her more of my time. Maybe even my undivided attention. The whole experience was a sensory overload filled with Carina and all of it was a good thing. Her smile when she turned shy, and her grin when she turned sexy. I was learning a hell of a lot without talking at all. But the concert was only the prelude to what became an extraordinary night. Carina is what I would call the perfect partner in bed, and possibly in life, for me. She was intelligent, kind, and sexy. She looked good, all full and luscious. She smelled fucking good. Like vanilla and heaven. She tasted good. Like honey and pleasure. She felt so damn good, my dick was getting hard again just thinking about it. Wet, juicy, thickness between her thighs. I wanted more of everything I encountered last night. That was why I stayed past coffee. I ended up staying another night at her place after spending the entire day with her.

I had to convince myself that I needed to leave the next morning. *Salik, let the woman do whatever it is women do when they are home alone. Play in their hair, clip their toes nails, something.* But when she stretched out and yawned bringing her beautiful tits closer to my face, I forgot my pep talk. Awww hell.

"You got plans today?"

She shook her head no while biting down on her plump lip. Her hair was all over the place because I couldn't let the woman out of my arms.

"You want me to leave?" I asked her. I held my breath as she stared back at me. Another head shake and shy smile was her response. I realized then that she didn't want to voice her desire for me to stay, probably because she didn't want to come off clingy, but here I was, wanting what she wanted. In my estimation, that makes for a perfect start.

"Then I'll stay," I told her.

CARINA

Salik and I were inseparable outside of work. With exception to his time at the gym and mine at yoga three evenings a week we were making a point to see each other and get to know one another. Even Saturday morning at his place, when I got up to shower to go home and do my laundry, he stopped me and shocked me with his request.

"Come with me to the barbershop."

I stopped dead in my tracks and walked back to front of his bed that he was still lying in. I already had to pry myself out of his ripped arms to even get up to shower and there he was, sprawled out with his sheet barely covering everything I had devoured just a few hours before.

"I thought women were forbidden from hanging around the barbershop."

He chuckled. "Nah, not really. Plenty of women need to bring their children in for haircuts anyway, so it's not like you'll be out of place in there."

I chewed on my lip and looked away from his seductive eyes. His lips, his entire body, seemed made for me and if I looked too long at any of those places, I'd be back in this bed and neither of us would make it to the barbershop.

"You there for just a haircut or to drop off some computers?" I looked him in his eyes and watched as a slow smile appeared on his handsome face because he knew he had gotten me. Goodness, how could any woman tell him no?

"Just a cut. Unless someone asks me for something, I'll be in and out."

"Alright, I'll go with you but after you're done, I *have* to get home to do this laundry. It's been piling up, and it's your fault."

He chuckled before placing his hands behind his head and relaxing back into his pillow.

"What have I done?"

"Everything."

I watched as he bit his lip. Then, under their own volition, my eyes traveled down the length of his rich brown body until that landed at the thatch of hair beneath his navel. Then, as if it sought my attention, his length stirred to life and thickened beneath the sheet, begging, taunting, and making it clear it wanted me.

"Okay, I'll go," I rushed to say.

Now he was laughing.

"Good, now come back in this bed with me. We've got time. I'll make sure of it."

I could lie to myself and say I started to move to his side of the bed and slid in beside him, strictly to avoid fussing so early in our ... whatever it was we were doing, but that would be a bald-faced lie. The truth was, I wanted to be with him, and he wanted me with him, so that was that.

As he pulled me into the warmth of his body, I felt safe and secure. Even as I reminded myself that it was too soon to hope so much—that what we were doing was too new, and I could get my feelings hurt. And as he kissed me and grabbed my ass before positioning me on my back, another part of me decided that I didn't care that I was moving too fast emotionally. When he parted my thighs and moved deeply inside of my wet body, my choked-out cry was me deciding to free myself from that worry, any worry. I decided instead to allow my hips and my mind to move freely with his as he continued to stir my passion. As he brought me to another orgasm, with his seductive whispers into my ear, I realized I had fallen stupidly in love with Salik. Salik, the man who had broken many hearts.

Later we walked into *Marlon's* to find it teeming with men and young boys waiting for their weekly fresh cut. I saw none of the mothers Salik promised would be there. Giving Salik a look, earned me a smile and shrug as he found me a corner to sit in.

"Marlon looks like he's ready for me," he whispered to me as he leaned over to talk to me, "I shouldn't be long at all." His eyes held a question. *Are you cool?* I nodded to let him know I was. My reward was a kiss on my lips before he stood up and walked over to his barber's chair.

His barber, Marlon, gave me a second glance as a few "damns" rang out. Of course, my face grew warm as I got the stares of almost everyone up in there. I could clobber Salik. He, however, seemed oblivious. Either he wasn't paying attention, or he did not care about the attention we were getting. Marlon's chair was situated near the back of the shop, with three other chairs closer to the front closer to the window and waiting area. Each chair was filled with a client, and each barber tending to that client, so it was impossible for me to know exactly what the conversation he seemed so enraptured in with Marlon, who would give him a few buzzes with the clippers around his nape, and then a few swipes with a brush before he would lean into Salik as if schooling him. Salik had mentioned to me on the drive over here, that it was Marlon that often gave him life advice as a young man, and that he was seen as a *Master Teacher* amongst the young black men of the community. Having had the same hairstylist, Tamera, for over a decade, and us having some deeply enriching conversations over the years, I could understand how a relationship with his barber would have the ability to shape him, and influence him.

Despite Salik's promise that he wouldn't be long, he took long enough that I got to witness a lot happening in this shop. Some clothes got sold, sports discussions got heated as they watched training camp talk on the mounted tv, and eventually a few mothers rolled in to pick up their sons. A couple looked like they were there to pick up more than their sons, but I couldn't knock the player or the game as long as they weren't there for Salik. About forty-five minutes later, Salik was getting out of Marlon's chair and paying him for his service. I grabbed my purse thinking he would be walking over to me so we could roll out but instead, he asked me to come back to meet Marlon.

"My barber wanted to say hi to you real quick and then I promise we'll go."

His eyes searched mine to see if I was still good and I was. I gave him a smile and walked past customers waiting for their turn.

"Mmmmhmmm, Salik got him a pretty one," I heard someone say.

"Yeah. He ain't never brought a woman around here. Next week the man gonna be married."

I ignored their voices even as my mind was doing flips at the realization that Salik hadn't brought other women here.

When we approached the light brown skin man with a low cut and neatly trimmed goatee, I noticed something immediately— Marlon had wise eyes.

"Carina, this is Marlon. Marlon, this is my lady, Carina." My eyes shot to Salik's and he just smiled.

I turned and shook Marlon's hand. "Salik has been coming in here since he was a teenager. You're his first lady. So, I had to meet cha. You from around here, Carina?"

"Not far. My family is from the Homewood-Point Breeze area, but I live in Lawrenceville now."

"Oh is that right? You're from round the way. Not far from this place. I don't care if those people call this place East Side Village. You and I both know it's *East Liberty*. Gentrification can't erase us as long as we keep telling our story. Hear me?"

"I do." I liked Marlon … a lot.

"Good. Well I'll let you get going. Salik said he had some laundry to do with you," I looked at Salik who shrugged, and then back at Marlon as he continued, "so I don't need to be holding you. But you keep him on his toes."

Chuckling, I nodded. "Yeah, I'll do that."

I watched the two men give each other daps before feeling Salik's hand reaching for mine. Eyes ogled, Even Marlon called out, "Go head Lik," but he didn't respond to them. He pulled me in closer and walked me out into the sunshine.

"Laundry, huh?" I looked up at him.

He shrugged again. "I'm not ready to leave you yet. You good with that?"

Without hesitation, I told him the truth. "I'm good with it."

I was more than good with it actually. It was perfect for me.

"Perfect." His words echoed my thoughts.

SALIK

I've always had the ability to keep my emotions in check when it came to the women I've been with. I had one semi-serious relationship a couple of years ago while in college. Her name was Qiana. Pretty, smart, great body, and sweet as could be. She was sweeter than I deserved probably. There was absolutely not a thing wrong with Qiana, only that we were going in different directions. She was moving to Texas to pursue a job she landed with her degree in engineering, and I wouldn't be leaving Pittsburgh, at least not yet. So, we separated which is what my mom warned would happen.

"Getting in relationships when you're in school is bound to lead to disappointment somehow. Either you're stuck with someone you fell in love with before you find out who you are, or you realize it before it's too late, and you go your separate ways with a broken heart."

At the time, I was sure my mom was wrong because Qiana was all I could think about, and she seemed to be feeling the same way about me. That was until she had the chance to take that job at the oil company in Houston, and then it was, "Salik, my future career is all that matters. I didn't come to school to end up married." She was right of course because neither did I. But damn, I had all I wanted in her, or so I thought. After many sexual conquests and a little bit of growing up, I could see now that I was just a boy with puppy dog love. I had a lot of growing up to do. Not that I had changed drastically, at least not on the surface, but my heart, my desires, had all shifted, and being with Carina was proof of that. It was early on in our relationship if you could call it that, because neither of us had made a commitment, but I was ready to. I was just afraid to scare her off. I was already counting myself lucky that she seemed to enjoy being around me as much as I loved being around her. Truthfully, it was more than that. We were compatible. Our vibe matched up; we could talk about any and everything, she made me laugh, she liked my jokes, we loved the same movies. Carina could cook and fuck any woman that came before her under the table, but even without all those other things, it was just her. I really *really* liked her, and that had no explanation.

The early morning hours before we got up for work, Carina lay in my arms, her hair spread out over my chest, her soft breaths tickling my skin, the side of her face over my heart. I pulled her in closer and breathed in the scent of the light perfume she wore. It was so mild you almost missed it, until she moved around in my arms, and I caught a whiff that made me want to pull her closer like I did this morning. She stretched against me, arching her back before settling back in and starting to snore again. I wanted her and hoped she knew it. So, I ran my palm down the smooth skin of her side, caressing her curves until I got to her sweet fucking ass and squeezed it. She murmured but remained in her dream. Another squeeze and she snored again, mumbling something incoherent. My dick was hard when her eyes fluttered open and focused on. Me.

"You okay?" she asked that her sexy, husky voice of hers.

I nodded and moved from under her allowing her to fall to her back, just the way I wanted.

AJA

She moaned when I leaned down to pull her dark brown nipple into my mouth—flicking it and sucking it until it grew hard inside my mouth. She twisted beneath me, whimpering, begging me to enter her.

I denied her request and moved to the twin peak and gave it attention until Carina reached for my dick and stroked me with her soft palm. My eyes closed. She knew how to touch me like a magician. Anything she wanted, she would get if she kept touching me so expertly. Proof of that was that I moved in between her thighs and placed them on my shoulders the way she loved it. My length sat at her slick opening, feeling the promise of the goodness to come. This woman was always ready for me. Ripe, warm, dripping all over my sheets without much foreplay from me even though she always got that from me.

I loved making her body beg for mine. *I loved this pussy, and her,* I thought as I thrust inside of heaven. Damn, she felt good. Her walls were soft, wet, and they were squeezing me like they loved the hell out of my dick. My breathing was all wrong for this occasion. If I didn't gain control, I would be out of this in a minute. She seemed to know it too. Our eyes connected, and her look was so soft. I'm just going to go ahead and admit that for the first time in my life I could see love in a woman's eyes. That should have scared me but it didn't. I just kept moving inside of her, connecting with her, loving her back. Her moans were my undoing, or maybe it was her hands clutching onto my back, and then on my ass begging me to swim deeper. I had to, or I would drown, but there was no control in this. I was gone, had fallen into the deepness of Carina. I could only hope that she would bring me back to shore when she was through.

It was a beautiful morning, but I found the day would take an ugly turn. One I wasn't looking forward to, not today, but had been expecting. Carina and I had been making breakfast at home a few days a week. Even if I came to get her from home when she didn't stay over, she was still handing me a healthy breakfast sandwich she was trying out, or a smoothie because she knew that was my favorite. She still loved Tony but her eating habits were changing due to some weight loss goals she had. From my perspective, every curve, jiggle, dimple that woman possessed was beautiful and all mine. I had no complaints loving on a fuller figured woman but I understood what she desired and respected it so I planned to help in any way I could.

Currently the plan was to help her burn her calories in bed. I could do that every day, no problem.

I was just about to dig into the sandwich she made me when I realized I was out of napkins at my desk. So I went to the break room to get some when I saw Dom in there by the refrigerator. Seeing her in her form-fitting dress, I was reminded of how my lusts used to get the best of me here. How my desire to see how she looked under her clothes led me to ask her out and how once I found out the answer to my question, I no longer cared what was beneath her clothes. Dom wasn't the problem back then. I had been, but this was now, and now she and her foul energy had the ability to bring me major problems at work. All week she had been giving off hostile vibes, so I knew it was boiling to the point of no return. I'd been avoiding her as much as possible, but there was only so much avoiding I could do with us working in the same department.

"Salik."

"Dom."

"What you and your girlfriend not eating together this morning?" This is when I pulled out my phone and acted like I was checking for something as I headed toward the condiments and paperware. I pressed record because something told me that I would need to. Actually, it was Marlon who gave me the advice. He said, "you might not be able to use it in court, but you for damn sure can use it to get your ass out of trouble at work."

When I turned back around to face Dom, she had her coffee mug in hand like she was about to leave.

"Why does what I do in my free time concern you, Dom? We aren't a couple. We *had* been friends, but this was never more than that."

"We fucked. You remember that?"

I took a deep breath. "I do, and that was long ago, and we both moved on. Well, I thought we did but now you're at work acting like I lied after making promises to you."

"You know what ... forget it," she was waving her hand like she couldn't take my shit no more. It was me that couldn't take *her* shit no more but I remained calm.

"I thought you could see that I wanted more." It was the first time she said something that struck a chord within me. Her eyes looked wounded, and honestly, confused.

So I leveled with her. "I'm sorry that I missed it. That I missed the signs of you wanting more but in the spirit of being honest, I would have never wanted more."

"Not with me."

"At the time, not with anyone."

She stared at me for a moment as if trying to assess whether my words were truthful. It didn't matter to me whether she believed they were. I just needed the drama to end.

"So what is it about her?" Sigh. Why do women go there?

Everything. That was what I wanted to say to her, but she had been hurt enough so I only said, "I don't know."

She sucked her teeth and her scowl returned. "Well, I hope you both get what you deserve together." And she walked out.

I breathed a sigh of relief when she was gone because I knew the conversation could have been so much worse. There could have been yelling. Could have been some dishes thrown too. Someone could have walked in. But when I ended the recording, I knew I had enough to protect myself if Dom ever made this fight uglier than it already was.

CARINA

Remember how I used to walk up in here still feeling frustrated after having Richie over? Well not no more. I now understood why some women I worked with would appear to be walking on cloud nine some mornings. All that positivity was coming from good dick. Who knew? More than that, the time I was spending with Salik was filled with more than sex. We laughed a lot. He was silly in a way that surprised me. Every time I saw him before knowing him, his expression was so serious that finding a man full of jokes was unexpected, but he had them and was seriously funny. Between laughing at his antics and watching corny movies with him, my cheeks hurt most days from the constant laughter. We also talked about almost everything; there wasn't a question I couldn't ask and while he wasn't as quick to dig deeper into every part of me, not in the way I dug in, his questions seemed more deliberate. He was taking his time while admittedly, I was ready to jump into a relationship. I know, I know, it was foolish of me to even be going this far in my mind and heart, but I was here. Too late to go back now.

"Well look at you. Got a big grin on your face," Tracey pointed out as she rounded the gray fabric-covered wall in my cube.

I slid my purse into my desk drawer, leaned against my desk with my hip, and crossed my arms. Then, shaking my head I had to ask her, "Whatever do you mean, Trace?"

"Oh, it's *Trace* now, is it? What kind of dick that man giving you?"

"Shhhhhh." I walked out of my partition and started looking around to see who else might have heard her.

"Girl, whether I yell it out or not, the whole world knows the two of you are together and happy to boot." I walked back into my cubicle and looked at her.

I didn't deny it. I couldn't.

"I'm happy for you."

"Thank you, Tracey. It's still new, so I –"

"No, don't do that. People get married and stay together for years and are miserable from day one until either of them dies. Some people get together and are happy for a while and then turn miserable. The length of a relationship is not at all an indicator of what's to come. That's why you allow yourself to be happy with every good moment." She sounded like Tori.

"Not sure what to say."

"Just say I'm right. Because I am."

"You're right." I chuckled and shook my head.

I plopped down into my chair and waited until she sat in the chair beside my desk. "What's up with you?"

"Nothing girl. I come to work. I go home and feed my cat. On a rare occasion I get asked out, I enjoy myself, maybe get a little bit of dick, and then go back to minding my business."

"Maybe the little bit of dick can become more if you let it, Trace."

"Uh uh, what we are not going to do is try to make a mountain out of every molehill. Sometimes dick is just dick."

"Sometimes, not all the time."

"Most of the time. How bout that?"

I couldn't argue with that, so I didn't. Her eyes told me she knew she had me.

"Not everyone finds the man of their dreams like you did—at work no less. You didn't even have to search far."

I chuckled. "That's not fair. How long did it take for him to even know who I was?"

"But it happened."

"Yeah but I'm good with me and Bubba."

She didn't sound at all sad about having a quieter life that only included her cat. If she loved it, I loved it for her.

"Bubba loves to eat."

"Don't he? Just as fat as me."

"Quit it. You just got a booty."

"That's all this sitting we do around here. That's why I come to talk to you every day. It's giving me exercise."

I laughed at that. "I understand. The yoga I've been doing is helping me out too."

"And Salik."

"And him, yes." I shook my head.

"I do have to warn you, though."

"About what?"

"That heffa, Dominique. I saw her talking to Sharise about you this morning. I know Sharise is on the committee for the opening you're going for upstairs, right?"

That bitch. "Yeah."

"Well, I don't know what was said but Sharise seemed really interested in what ol' heffa had to say."

"Which is a damn shame."

I wouldn't say more because Dominique wasn't just a problem for me. She was a problem for Salik as well and me telling Tracey about Dominique would be also telling Salik's business. Which I just would not do. However, I had to wonder what Dominique was doing talking to Sharise. If she even attempted to get in the way of me and that promotion, I'm not sure I'll be able to keep my job here because Dominique and her beautiful weave will be all over the concrete outside this building.

Tracey chattered on for a while. Most of it I missed because my mind was all over the place. I knew there were multiple women that knew about Salik and I, and those same women were upset that I was apparently more than a notch on his bed post but they only gave me side eyes and kept it moving. Dom was another story, however. She was downright hostile whenever we saw each other. All these years of not even knowing who the hell she was, and suddenly I ran into her left and right, which told me she was making sure of it. The way she was acting, you'd think he broke off an engagement to get with me.

Salik shared with me what kind of relationship he had had with Dominique in the past and how he thought they could continue to be friends afterward. Little did he know she had fallen in love with him the way all the rest of the women had, which was why she was jealous when she ran into the two of us after our first lunch at *Trello's*. He also told me how he had a revelation, and it was at that moment, he decided that he wanted to pursue me. His honesty is why I continued to want to see him despite my worry about office drama. But now office drama was about to be my drama.

After Tracey left, I went to work until my eyes needed a break, and then I pulled my phone out of my desk. There were two missed calls from Salik and a text telling me to get in touch.

I dialed him up and as soon as the call connected, he answered.

"If you can get away, meet me at my car. I have something to tell you."

I didn't even question the urgency; I could hear it in his voice.

I told Pat I needed to take a short break if Sharise came around and I rolled out, took the elevators down and walked out to the parking lot that KIB owned. Salik was on level three, which I knew because we came into work together this day and for the past few weeks. He usually parked in the same spot because there was a huge slate concrete pillar that hid us from view when we spent a few minutes kissing and touching. I found him leaning against that pillar, looking his usual fine self, but my steps slowed when I really took him in. His posture, his eyes, said he was more than tired. He was exhausted.

"What's wrong?"

"Dominique."

"What about her?" My heart started pounding. I'd been worried about what she might do, especially to him in his job.

"She went to Sarah and told her that I sexually assaulted her. That that was the real reason we were arguing. Because she was threatening to tell, and I didn't want her to."

"What the hell!"

"Yeah, but your man is wise." My heart skipped at his "my man" statement but I let him continue.

"I recorded the discussion I had with her an hour

before Sarah pulled me in with her to tell me about the complaint."

"What made you do that?"

"I told you she keeps sneering at me. Ain't no way she wasn't going to be up to something. So when I saw her in the break room, I pushed the button and waited for her to start talking."

"She is simple-minded. How did she really think she would get away with this?"

"Because a lot of people do. All they know is lies. I was sicka her shit, though."

I shook my head. "I was worried something else happened. Like a real confrontation with her."

"I've been trying to avoid anything going too far. One shouting match at work is enough to last me a lifetime."

"I can understand that. What will you do with the recording?"

"You mean what *did* I do with it."

I shook my head at him and smiled. "Yes, *did*."

"I gave it to Khalil. I mean, Mr. Berry."

"That's alright. I know you two have conversations with each other from time to time. Especially now that the integration went live. I like that you and John got some shout-outs from Mr. Berry in that companywide email too."

"Me too. More so for John because he stayed on my ass when I was tired of Sarah's constant changes."

"I think she just wants you to be the best."

He nodded. "I'm starting to think that too."

"What happens with Dominique now. Did Mr. Berry say?" I couldn't help to wonder how the timing of this was perfect considering it seemed Dominique was trying to sabotage my career.

"Khalil said he would handle it. That's all I know. It's all I care about too."

I shook my head. "It's so crazy to me that us going out could cause this much drama."

I watched as he stood up straight and put his arms out for me to move into. His body heat surrounded me as his arms wrapped around my body. It wasn't just how Salik talked to me, or even how he looked at me. The way he touched me told me he loved the way I felt.

"You think all of this happened because we are going out?"

I shrugged. "What else could it be?"

His finger went to my chin and lifted it so I could focus on his eyes, and his next words.

"Maybe it's love, Carina."

Before I could ask him what he meant or even

return the words back to him, he was kissing me. I didn't worry about anyone seeing us this time or about how we seemed to be happening so fast. As Tracey had said, I needed to enjoy each good moment while it was here.

EPILOGUE

 month later ...

I LOOKED over at the man I'd fallen in love with. His hand glided along the wheel of his truck as he made the turn to get onto the Turnpike taking us back to Pittsburgh. He had a gentle driving style that relaxed me, so I knew it wouldn't be long before I drifted off to sleep. Between staying up to watch preseason football with him, then playing Madden with him, which of course he won, to cuddling with him while watching Godfather, neither of us got much sleep the night before. That should have been reason enough for him to allow me to sleep in, but no, before the sky was splashed with orange, his dick was poking me in my ass asking to get some. And I obliged because why would I not? And then we had to get ready and get on the road to head out to a party in the damn country. So yeah, we were both a little tired. As if he felt me looking at him, he turned to me and winked.

"I'm happy you got the job, babe." He had taken to calling me babe. Sometimes he called me Goddess, but that was usually when we were home; mine or his.

"Me too. If they had given it to Charlene Plasky, I might have had to hit up your boy *Khalil* to set it all straight."

His deep chuckle made my toes curl inside of my brown peep-toe pumps. "We aren't *that* cool. Quit it."

"Oh yeah? Then why are we driving away from his country cottage on a Saturday?"

"Because he was having a celebration for the new *Soul Life* app, and other employees were there too, Carina."

"Uh huh, the top guys. No one else from your department was there. Not even John was invited to Khalil Berry's house. Just admit it, you are becoming friends, or maybe he's like a big brother."

I looked over at him. His eyes were still trained

on the road, but he smiled at that. "Yeah maybe. I don't mind having a mentor."

"I think it's dope that he would even take the time to care about your future."

"I do too, babe."

The past month was like a whirlwind. After Khalil Berry reviewed the recording of Dominique admitting she and Salik had had a consensual encounter over a year before, Khalil spoke to Sarah and HR. The decision was made that since Dominique made false statements against Salik, she diminished trust with the company and would be terminated. Salik could press charges if he wanted which he decided against because he really wanted that chapter to be over.

Sharise also lost her job as department head because as Dominique was being fired, she admitted that she and Sharise were trying to find a way to move me out of the hiring pool for the software developer position. It seemed she wanted me to stay put. I still couldn't for the life of me, understand why Sharise would ruin her career for Dom, but some things weren't meant to be understood like my mom would say to me.

Still riding on the high from my promotion, Salik was then invited to attend a semi-private celebration at Khalil's country estate. He immediately invited me to be his plus one. For a few hours, we got to spend time with Khalil and his family. His wife, Zola, was probably the most luminous woman I had ever met, even seven months pregnant with their second child. Matter of fact, all of Khalil's in-laws were there, and the women all had this glow about them that was hard to ignore. Also, their eyes held some kind of mysticism in them that didn't spook me out like it could have. Instead, I was drawn to it. I wanted to sit at the older woman's feet and listen to her tell stories about our ancestors. She was Khalil's mother-in-law, Zora, I learned.

"Did you notice how beautiful Khalil's family is?"

"Babe, I don't look at stuff like that." He chuckled.

"Yeah yeah. How could you not notice them? And their babies! So adorable. All boys."

"You sound like you want children."

We had never ventured this far into what we wanted with our futures. I wasn't sure how he felt about having children or even getting married one day. I made sure to stay away from discussing it because I didn't want to spook him off. It was way too soon to talk marriage with him. His mother seemed to think I was the one, however. When he brought me home to meet her, his aunts, and his brothers, she made sure to tell me she wanted me to be her daughter in law. I smiled shyly and caught a glimpse of Salik to see what his reaction was. He only winked at me before going back to the preseason game he and his brothers were watching. Men.

"I wouldn't mind having a large family one day."

"I wouldn't either." I looked over at him, and for a moment, he took his eyes off the road to look at me before giving his attention back to his driving.

The next song on the playlist Salik made for this trip came on. Sade's *By Your Side* came in smooth. The perfect tone for this moment right now. He always knew how to give me the best experience in the car. The playlists were something he started creating for me a couple of months ago so the moment I got in his car, I would hear the music that made him think of me when we were apart.

Oh, when you're cold
   I'll be there, hold you tight to me

. . .

I TOOK A DEEP BREATH. The entire day felt different. Like he and I were shifting into something new, but I was too afraid to analyze that or even bring it up. But his question made me wonder if there was a future and whether I'd have to be the one to bring it up or would it just happen naturally, organically, because he wanted what I wanted. And then his voice broke the silence.

"What do you think is next for us?" He asked.

My eyes that had drifted close opened and I looked over at him.

"Us as in ..." I held my breath.

"Us. Carina and Salik." His hand reached across the console, and I immediately met his hand with mine and entwined my fingers with his. For the first time in my life, a man wanted to know what was next with us. Not me searching for more or begging for someone to love me as much as I loved them. No, for once, a man loved me and wanted a future.

"Whether you want to be next, I'm all for it. I love you, Salik."

"And I love you, my Goddess."

ALSO BY AJA

For Once

She's Got Soul

Deep In My Soul

Soul Love

Soul Ties

Enigma

Tease

Allure

Sizzle

Santa's Baby

I Am Yours

One Night

Good Old Soul

Love's Required

Love Taps

Anything For You

The Swan

Where Hope Grows

ABOUT THE AUTHOR

Aja is an Award-Winning National Best-Selling author of passionate women's fiction & romance. Readers experience realistic, passionate, and soulful interactions with her work. She is inspired by soulful music and sensual art and uses them to help craft her stories.

Aja is the recipient of multiple awards including BRAB's Beverly Jenkins Author of The Year Award for 2020. When she's not being a wife and mother, you can find her looking for a spot on the beach to watch the sunrise over the remarkable waves.

www.ajathewriter.com

Made in United States
Orlando, FL
01 May 2022